The Bachura Scandal

and other stories and sketches

The translator, Alan Menhennet, is Professor of German at
the University of Newcastle upon Tyne, where he also
teaches Austrian/Czech history.

JAROSLAV HAŠEK

The Bachura Scandal

and other stories and sketches

Translated from the Czech with an Introduction by
Alan Menhennet

ANGEL BOOKS
London

Dedicated to
Everill Waters Menhennet

and in memory of
Thomas William Menhennet

First published 1991 by
Angel Books, 3 Kelross Road, London N5 2QS

Translation and Introduction © Alan Menhennet 1991

British Library Cataloguing-in-Publication Data:

A catalogue record for this book is available
from the British Library

ISBN 0 946162 41 7 pbk

This book is printed on Permanent Paper conforming
to the British Library recommendations and to the
full American standard

Typeset in Great Britain by EMS Photosetters, Thorpe Bay, Essex
Printed and bound by Woolnough Bookbinding,
Irthlingborough, Northants

Contents

Introduction

Jaroslav Hašek was born in Prague on 30 April 1883. The inexorable but absurd logic that governs the lives of so many of his characters presided over his birth as well, for he was born both a Czech and an Austrian and lived for the greater part of his life under the authority of the strange two-headed beast that was the Habsburg Empire. Prague was the Czech capital, but it was a 'provincial Austrian city'[1] and its administration was that of the strictly 'Austrian' (that is, spiritually if not necessarily linguistically 'German') part of the Austro-Hungarian state. During the course of the nineteenth century, the Czechs had managed to revive and rebuild their national consciousness.[2] Yet it is the Austrian customs through which the Czech traveller in the story of that name, who is returning from a Saxony which directly borders Bohemia, has to pass, and whose regulations will permit him to set foot in his *vlast*, his homeland, only if he agrees to the removal of one of his kidneys. The bumbling petty bourgeois benefactor Mr Kauble, when confronted by a visiting dignitary who embodies the state, speaks, 'like a good Czech', in German.

A good Czech, from the Habsburg point of view, was an Austrian Czech. Whether the local Sheriff or the customs official spoke Czech or German, he *thought* German and felt the allegiance to the German dynasty, and its black-and-gold colours, that informed the principal arms of the state, its civil service and its officer-corps. Hašek reserves his most hilarious and often savage satire for the 'loyal' Czech, such as the egregious Lieutenant Dub in *The Fortunes of the Good Soldier Schweik* (1921–3) or the toll-collector Štěpán Brych, who sacrifices his own life, as well as that of a mere 'civilian', in order that the statutory kreuzer should be rendered unto the Emperor.

Hašek's home circumstances were middle-class, but rather precariously so. His father, an alcoholic, worked in relatively low-paid teaching and banking jobs and died in 1896. His mother seems to have been unable to provide the parental discipline that he clearly needed. He had started well at grammar-school, but both his performance and his behaviour deteriorated and after several brushes with the police, he was expelled. On one occasion, the police had found his pockets stuffed full of stones (which he claimed were part of the school's geological collection), a fragment of his biography which reappears (as do many others) in one of his stories (*The Coffin-Dealer*). Hašek cannot, to be sure, be absolved from all blame for the false starts and failures of his own life, yet here too, we do seem at times to detect the amoral principle of cussedness and inconsequentiality that rules in his comic writing: as if he were sometimes naïvely acting out the comedy of life by following momentary impulses. One wonders, for example, whether he had a clear intention in his mind when in 1911, after the break with Jarmila, he climbed the parapet of the Charles Bridge (the incident reflected in *A Psychiatric Puzzle*), to claim afterwards that he wanted to be sick into the river rather than on the pavement in front of Saint John Nepomuk.[3]

A job with a chemist did not last long and a second chemist suggested to his mother that his place was at the Czechoslavonic Commercial Academy, where, not without distinction, he completed his education from 1899 to 1902. By this time, his career as a writer had already begun. A number of stories, based mainly on his travels on foot around some of the farther-flung outposts of the Empire, had appeared in a variety of journals. Hašek mixed briefly in avant-garde literary circles but while drinking and talking in pubs and cafés was much to his taste – and remained so – he was out of sympathy with the aesthetic mode of thought. He was a born writer, but an anti-'poetic' one by nature.

Ideally suited to the bohemian life, Hašek was, to use Cecil Parrott's phrase, a 'Bad Bohemian'[4] as far as his social existence was concerned. After overlooking one period of absence without leave, the Slavie Bank sacked him on the second occasion, in 1903. Between 1904 and 1906, the nearest he seems to have come to a settled occupation was his involvement with the anarchist movement. His general sympathies were with the radical left and he would no doubt have felt a certain temperamental affinity with anarchism, but it is doubtful whether he had firm anarchist convictions and he eventually detached himself from this rather dubious company and spent some time travelling, · most notably in Bavaria, where he no doubt met the prototype of his *Tourist Guide*.

In 1906, he fell in love with Jarmila Mayerová and she with him. Her parents had their doubts as to his suitability as a son-in-law and it was not until 1910 that he was able to overcome their resistance. In the interim, he flirted intermittently with anarchism, got himself arrested and indulged his penchant for turning life as well as art into caricature as campaign-manager for the National Social Party during a Prague by-election in 1908. He was particularly hard on the traditional nationalist party, the Young Czechs, which clearly took itself and the conventional political game too seriously for his taste. One of its leading activists, Milada Sisová, was guyed as the 'Czech Maid of Orleans'. She reappears in this role in the story *Election Day in the Malá Strana*.[5]

Thanks to the good offices of his friend Ladislav Hájek, he obtained a post on the staff of the magazine *Animal World* and inherited the editorship from Hájek in due course. On the strength of this, he was married to Jarmila, but regular employment and settled married bliss were of short duration. An inveterate hoaxer and prankster, Hašek found the purveying of true facts about real animals too boring and treated his readers to more exotic fare. Elephants, they were no doubt intrigued to learn, like to hear music played on the gramophone; tigers, on the other hand, do not. The fossil of an 'antediluvian flea' was solemnly 'discovered'. The last straw was the special offer of a pair of thoroughbred werewolves. Once again, Hašek found himself without a job and a 'Cynological Institute' (Hašek's pseudo-scientific designation of his activities as a dog-dealer) founded soon afterwards also failed in short order. Both episodes were most fruitful as material for stories and for episodes in *Schweik*. The marriage broke down, though not terminally, and Jarmila went back to live with her parents.

It was in this year (1911) that the 'suicide-attempt' on the Charles Bridge took place, and that Hašek perpetrated his greatest hoax, as the mock-candidate of a spoof-party, the 'Party for Moderate Progress Within the Limits of the Law', in the Prague district of Vinohrady. The meetings, at which he made witty and scurrilous impromptu speeches, were held in a pub and the manifesto contained such proposals as the nationalisation of concierges and the 'rehabilitation of animals'. The use of animal-names in abusive language was to be prohibited: an ox, at 700 kilos, was of more importance than a parliamentary candidate at about 80. Hašek then wrote a mock-serious *History* of the party which was so full of slanderous remarks and portraits that although it was ready in 1912, it was not published in full until many years after the author's death.

When he was called up in 1915, Hašek joined the 91st Infantry Regiment and eventually arrived at the Galician front, where he was taken prisoner by the Russians, then released and allowed to join the Czech Legion. He worked for a time for *Čechoslovan*, the organ of a conservative group of Pan-Slav orientation which was based in Kiev, and it was there, in 1916, that the last of the stories in this selection appeared.

The rest of Hašek's career may be summarised briefly. He deserted from the Legion after 1917 and joined the Bolsheviks, whose strict discipline enabled him to stop drinking for a time and with whom he seems to have felt genuinely at home. He rose to positions of some prominence in the Russian Communist Party, and in 1920 was sent back to the newly established Czech Republic, with a Russian wife whom he had bigamously acquired along the way, presumably to work for the Communist cause. But there was little chance of progress in that direction and in any case, old habits returned with his return home. But as a double deserter, he was generally suspect. And he was no longer capable of a sustained bohemian existence. He became depressed and generally out of sorts. And then came the inspiration of turning Schweik, who had first made his appearance in a series of (not very inspired) pre-war short stories, into the 'hero' of a full-length novel. He spent the last two years of his life in Lipnice, in the Bohemian–Moravian highlands, writing *Schweik* and growing progressively more unhealthy. He died with his masterpiece still unfinished.

Hašek as a satirist is, as Robert Pynsent has shown,[6] but one among many in a rich Czech tradition. The targets of his satire are the predictable ones and are attacked effectively enough.[7] But Hašek the humorist is a different matter. It is in this capacity that he speaks to us, not about life as it is or ought to be, which (for all their recognition of the grotesque side) seems to be the view of him taken by the Communist critics,[8] but about Life. By this, I mean the force which lies latent in our carefully constructed and ordered reality and is always capable, often hilariously, but often also savagely, even frighteningly, of disrupting that order. And it is necessary as well as natural that it should do so, for deliberately or not, this order of ours often suppresses freedom. It is this force that informs Hašek's humour at its most characteristic. And it is its presence that helps to explain why his crassness, his frequent bad taste and his disregard of the aesthetic niceties do not rule him out of consideration as a writer of importance.

That *The Bachura Scandal* should centre on a urinal and a public convenience is, primarily at least, not some kind of symbolism, neither is it the result of a simple taste for the cloacal. The effect is that of the defeat of the spirit of convention and organised procedure. In *Robbery and Murder in Court*, the story of a man who is patently a victim of society in the classic satirical sense is concluded not with a cry of rage, not with a sentimental whimper, but with a fart as the order of the courtroom, which has been teetering on the brink throughout, finally subsides like a punctured balloon.

There is a direct relationship between the form of Hašek's stories and their substance. They were, of course, *feuilletons*, written for money and written at speed. But such journalistic considerations do not necessarily rule out a sense of form and in particular, as many a practised piece in the 'quality' newspapers can demonstrate, the gentle art of the rounded conclusion. Hašek's stories, however, do not so much end as stop. His *modus operandi* as a contributor to the journal *Tribuna* is revealing.[9] He would turn up at the offices with nothing written, whereupon the routine was to lock him into a room with paper, pencil and one glass of beer. Eventually, he would emerge, hand over some sheets covered in neat, 'rather childish' writing and ask '*Je toho dost?*' (Is that enough?), pocket the advance for his next piece and go on his way. He was turning on a tap, letting it run for what seemed an appropriate period and then shutting it off.

Viewed aesthetically, Hašek's conclusions are sometimes clumsy and peremptory. He simply kills off a character, packs him off to an asylum or has him faint, as in *The Demon Barber of Prague*. But the true ending is the open ending which is often clearly visible through such ostensible 'conclusions'. The unity of these stories derives from the fact that they all belong to a gigantic tapestry and running through this, visible only in its effects, is the comic law.

Just as honesty is 'for rich folk', as the lumberman says in *The Struggle for Souls*, so heroism is for the world of seriousness, respectability and tragedy. Chocholka, the dunce who flees from the Latin test into the toilet and whose desperate defence of this last redoubt is linked with Thermopylae, is no hero. He acts by instinct (as Schweik often does) and becomes the involuntary vehicle of the spirit of humour. A consistent, programmatic anarchism, life spent entirely in the madhouse, would not have been what Hašek wanted. Maybe the attraction that Communism in revolutionary Russia held for him had to do with a feeling that here, order could at last be blended with freedom. He would not have been the only one to make such a mistake. The 'Bugulma' stories written during his period as a 'Commissar' in Russia show him in his own persona (as 'Gashek', for the Russians have no *h*), trying to create an idyll, to make order grow out of disorder.

At his most characteristic and effective though, Hašek deals in a reality that blends into phantasmagoria, albeit in a way very different from that of that other great Prague storyteller, Kafka. Chaos is needed in Hašek as a corrective to a world of order which is something of a prison-house and in which the price of freedom is eternal comic vigilance. It is a world in which one has to struggle in order to avoid being sucked down, as Štěpán Brych already has been before the story begins, into a whirlpool in which life is no more than the fulfilment of some official' role. Not that freedom automatically confers safety: in Hašek, neither mouse nor man can be entirely safe. But it does confer the gift of laughter, and through all the deaths and disasters of these stories, that is the sound most frequently heard: the essentially positive response of a comic writer to a comic world.

Notes

1   Cf. Robert Pynsent, 'Jaroslav Hašek' in *European Writers. The Twentieth Century* (ed. George Stade), New York, 1989, p. 1092.
2   Led in the initial stages by the cultural and political 'Awakeners', many of whom, notably Karel Havlíček (1821–56), are mentioned in *A Sporting Sketch*, and then by the 'Old Czech' and 'Young Czech' parties, the movement had succeeded within Bohemia in reestablishing a strong Czech cultural, commercial and political life. It failed, however, to make substantive progress at the national 'Austrian' level.
3   See E. A. Longen (E. A. Pitterman), *Můj Přítel Jaroslav Hašek*, Prague, 1983, p. 30.
4   See Cecil Parrott, *The Bad Bohemian. The Life of Jaroslav Hašek, Creator of the Good Soldier Švejk*, London, 1978.
5   And again in the *History of the Party for Moderate Progress Within the Limits of the Law*, where, on account of her gruff voice, she is mistaken for a man.
6   Op. cit., p. 1096.
7   They are discussed at length by Cecil Parrott, *Jaroslav Hašek. A Study of Švejk and the Short Stories*, Cambridge, 1982, pp. 75ff.
8   See, for example, Jiři Hájek, *Jaroslav Hašek*, Prague, 1983, pp. 109ff. and Radko Pytlík, *Jaroslav Hašek and the Good Soldier Schweik* (translated by David Short), Prague, 1982, especially pp. 20, 43–4 and 77, where the reactions of Hašek and Kafka to the 'absurdity' of the modern world are distinguished on the basis of the former's discovery of 'the solid reality and variety of life'.
9   I owe this anecdote to Professor J. P. Stern.

A Note on the Translation

All foreign literature has the potential to become English as well. This is land not so much 'conquered' as reclaimed. The result should be a new field that is genuinely English, and yet also to some degree still and forever 'foreign'. My aim has been to allow Hašek to remain a Czech and at the same time to live and breathe freely in an authentically English climate. The Czech context, above all the names and titles, has therefore been left largely unaltered, except where it seemed that not to change them would produce a stiff and un-English effect. To anglicise Mladá Boleslav, for example, or to give the old German name ('Jungbunzlau'), would have meant a loss of the Czech spirit with no obvious compensation: the body would still be a foreign one. To insist on 'Plzeň' instead of the familiar 'Pilsen' would, on the other hand, be mere pedantry. A certain eclecticism is necessary if one is to remain on the tightrope: what works best as English usage, while remaining foreign currency, seems to offer our best chance, even if this means that we must oscillate between crowns and kreutzers. I have tried to walk a tightrope, then, and no translator of Jaroslav Hašek can remain in any doubt as to the likely outcome of such an attempt. Naturally, I should prefer not to have fallen off, as I no doubt have from time to time. But I am not sure that I ought to apologise for this: it may well have added to the fun in a manner that Hašek himself would have appreciated.

Fidelity is the translator's mistress: but fidelity to what? A stiff, formal Hašek who loses his vitality and freedom in his new environment would be the greatest infidelity of all. In translating the great Taker of Liberties I have myself felt the need to take liberties and it will be for the reader, specialist and non-specialist alike, to decide whether these are justified. In rendering *U holiče* ('At the Barber's') as *The Demon Barber of Prague*, can I claim to have been true to the spirit of my original? It seemed to me a legitimate English response to the demonic quality of the original and I succumbed to the temptation, as I felt Hašek might have done, had Sweeney Todd been a Czech. This plea for freedom is not meant as an excuse for any mistakes that the translation might still contain.

The text used in this translation is that contained in the three volumes of the Selected Works designated as the 'First', 'Second' and 'Third Decameron' (Prague, Český Spisovatel, 1976–9, principal editor Radko Pytlík).

Eight of the thirty-two stories contained in this volume have already appeared in English translation, in the collection *The Tourist Guide* (Prague, Artia, 1961; translated by I. T. Havlů). Although these renderings are all too often inadequate as English, it would be churlish not to acknowledge that they also have their felicities and that I have profited greatly from consulting them. The stories involved are *The Sad Fate of the Station Mission*, *The Unfortunate Affair of the Tom-Cat*,* *Mr Florentin vs Chocholka*, *The Austrian Customs*, *Šejba the Burglar Goes on a Job*, *The Battle for Souls*, *The Tourist Guide* and *The Bachura Scandal*. They were simply too good to be left out.

To the best of my knowledge, all the other stories in this volume appear in English for the first time.

The stories are arranged in order of first publication (as far as can be ascertained).

---

* Also included in *Little Stories by a Great Master* (Prague, Orbis Press Agency, 1984; translated by Doris Kožíšková), a brief selection of Hašek's political satire.

Acknowledgements

My thanks are gratefully given to Professor Peter Stern and Dr David Short for material assistance, to Antony Wood for valuable suggestions, and to Rene Read for constant encouragement, a sympathetic ear and a great deal of sound advice.

Alan Menhennet
Newcastle upon Tyne, 1991

Robbery and Murder in Court

All the newspapers were at one in declaring that the criminal before the court was the kind of fellow that every decent person ought to avoid. For this scoundrel had committed robbery and murder. And now he was looking forward to his future with resignation, saying himself that he was bound for the gallows and punctuating the trial with gallows-humour in very bad taste. He prophesied to the State Prosecutor, for instance, that he too would be hanged one day.

Among other things, he also said that he would make a present of the rope with which he was to be hanged to the Presiding Judge, so that he could use it to keep his trousers up. These remarks naturally aroused the considerable displeasure of the Associate Judges and led to a dispute between the State Prosecutor and Defence Counsel, who maintained that the law, in its charity, gave to every accused the right to tell the court, as best he could, what he had on his mind. If the accused mentioned the Presiding Judge's trousers, he said, it was because he was clutching at a last straw in his own defence; he was trying to enlist the sympathies of the jury with this gallows-humour of his. The trousers . . .

At this point, Defence Counsel was interrupted by the State Prosecutor, who objected to this line of argument that to drag the Presiding Judge's trousers into the debate was immoral. To which Defence Counsel made the witty retort that it was not the trousers worn by the Presiding Judge that were immoral, it was the man inside them. The whole judicial system, he said, was immoral, from the jailer to the hangman. After this outburst, Defence Counsel was ruled out of order and a spittoon was brought, so that the Presiding Judge could relieve his feelings. The expectorations of the Presiding Judge caused a great stir in the courtroom. A number of ladies fainted and one spectator put his hand by mistake into a pocket that did not belong to him and drew out a piece of chocolate, at which he began to nibble nervously before the very eyes of the man whom he had robbed. An adjournment was called, of which the murderer and robber in the dock took advantage to make obscene gestures at the State Prosecutor.

After the adjournment, the trial was continued. It was brought to the notice of the court that the robber and murderer had carried out his crime with more than usual brutality. Before committing the act, he had not eaten for three days, so that he might now be able to maintain that he had stolen the loaf of bread which was the nub of the case out of hunger. What he had done went beyond all normal concepts of depravity. As he was in the act of stealing that loaf, the merchant whose rights he was violating had shot at him with his revolver and then they had grappled with one another and the merchant had been choked in the struggle. The murderer had fled, but on account of the large amount of blood he had lost, had soon fallen and been immediately taken by the gendarmes. His excuse, that he had acted in self-defence, was extremely inept. Why, for God's sake, hadn't he just stood there quietly and let himself be shot, shot dead if that was what it came to, when he had said under interrogation that a long time before he went on this job he had had thoughts of suicide?

A touching scene occurred when he was confronted with the wife of the murdered man, who spoke through her tears of the brutality of the crime. 'He choked him so hard, the poor man's eyes popped out of their sockets.' These few words from a simple woman sent a deep chill through all who heard them and one reporter made a note of the phrase 'Eyes Pop Out' for use as a column-heading in his report of the trial.

The accused himself made the impression of a criminal. He stated that he did not believe in God; Gawd could kiss his backside, he said, what had Gawd ever done for him? His grandfather, he went on, had died of hunger; his grandmother had been raped by a Captain of Gendarmes: in short, every word the man spoke produced a bad impression. The State Prosecutor asked permission to enter additional charges of disrespect for religion and disrespect for the army, for the Captain of Gendarmes had belonged to the militia. 'And I would add,' said the State Prosecutor, 'that in my opinion, the Captain of Gendarmes would never have raped the grandmother of the accused if he had known what sort of grandson he was going to have.'

This phrase aroused a strong reaction among the public and a number of ladies burst out crying, just as if the Captain of Gendarmes had violated them in person. At this, the criminal smiled 'in a self-satisfied manner' (this is the exact expression used in the court record) and it was plain to see that he was mocking the public and the majesty of the law. Under examination, he came out with objectionable pronouncements, such as: 'What d'you want me to do, then? Let 'im do me in?' and: 'So I give 'im a bit of a shake, silly old bugger; 'ow can I 'elp it if 'e drops down dead?' And more of the same.

Defence Counsel tried once or twice to win the jury over with brief explanations and appeals to their sympathy. But he was flogging a dead horse. All the jurors, as they gazed at the robber and murderer, were thirsting for blood. One of them wore a particularly bloodthirsty look. He hung on every word as the villain's jokes got coarser and coarser. That juror devoured the robber with his eyes, so to speak. At last he could contain himself no longer and shouted out: 'Is it giving you a kick, then, to think you're going to be hanged?'

To which tricky question the robber calmly replied: 'Not 'alf as much of a kick as it's giving you!'

At this pronouncement, the State Prosecutor rose and announced amid a deathly hush that he was going to wash his hands. He had, he said, eaten pickled herring during the adjournment. But this was just a pretext for this latter-day Pilate to go and pass water. He came back beaming all over his face like any man who has just taken a weight off his mind and seemed more kindly disposed to the accused than he had been before. Now, he no longer spat into his handkerchief every time he looked at the robber.

The examination of the witnesses confirmed the charge in every particular. It became clear that the accused had made a bad impression on everyone beforehand. Nor did it help his cause when it emerged that he was illegitimate and that he drank rye-brandy. 'I can't drink cognac,' the accused volunteered. At these words, the Presiding Judge ordered that the prisoner be removed, but he was brought back on an intervention by the defence. This episode did not pass without an emotional scene. As he was being taken out, the villain repeated emphatically: 'I can't drink cognac; I can't afford it!' Great excitement among the jury. 'If he could afford to drink it, he would,' one juror remarked. A storm of applause from the public gallery and shouts of: 'Old brandy-vat!' A call of 'Really!' from the jury. General uproar. A heckler is ejected by the prison guards. A call from the Presiding Judge: 'Where do you think you are, in a theatre?'

When the accused was brought back, he was confronted with the loaf of bread he had stolen and shown a picture of the murdered man. 'Is that the loaf?' asked the Presiding Judge. 'Yes,' said this hardened criminal without a tremor. 'Do you recognise your victim?' 'When I throttled him in the struggle, he was older than that.' This cynical reply had a profound effect on all who heard it; the toughest court-officials were shaken to the core.

Further witnesses made things still worse for the accused. Defence Counsel, who protested at this, was overruled by the Presiding Judge, who said that the witnesses were not being called for fun.* It was established by these witnesses that the criminal had nowhere to sleep. The causes of this phenomenon were not investigated further, but it was stated in addition that if he had nowhere to sleep, he might at least sleep somewhere other than in the church gardens. Another witness said that the robber and murderer had not worn a collar, another confirmed that he hadn't a shirt and one swore on oath that the murderer didn't know what a bar of soap was. What made things tightest of all for the accused was the testimony of the Mayor of his own home community, which was as follows: 'The ruffian never wore any socks, wiped his nose on his sleeve from the time that he was a boy, wrote filthy words on a placard meant for a procession, called the Mayor a pig twenty years ago and still owes him, the Mayor that is, twenty kreuzers.'

In the Jury-Room

'Gentlemen,' said one juror, when they had been called together to decide the fate of the accused. 'There isn't a place in all this town where you can get a decent bit of paprika. The accused is a worthless specimen. I got myself a portion of paprika at Dvořáks', and it wasn't fit to eat. Ever since he was a boy, he's been a confirmed liar and he's rounded off his career with a murder. I found a fly in that paprika. There's veal – and there's veal. That no-good lout killed a decent, hard-working man, a man who had devoted his whole life to the good of the community, a man, a respectable businessman, who would never have sold the kind of paprika they put in the sauce at Dvořáks'. A man who, if he had been a butcher, would never have had the neck to sell that ready-wrapped meat they used for the paprika I ate at Dvořáks' this morning. To the gallows with him, the scoundrel; let him swing, let him writhe in his death-agony! Only an out-and-out crook would charge thirty-five kreuzers for a portion that size. The man you have seen and whose deeds you are judging is a villain of the deepest dye. Steer clear of the Dvořáks' Restaurant, gentlemen! I give my vote and I say: "Is he guilty? Yes!" And you, gentlemen, what do you say?'

---

* Experience has shown that fun is precisely what witnesses *are* called for. [J. H.]

'Yes! – Yes! – Yes! – Yes! – Yes! – Yes! – Yes! – Yes! – Yes! – Yes! – Yes!'

'. . . To death by hanging,' the Presiding Judge read out the verdict. 'To death by hanging in the name of His Imperial Majesty,' he repeated. And then the ladies in the courtroom blew kisses to the gentlemen of the jury and the accused emitted a sound which was hardly the stuff of legend, but belonged rather to that category of subject which is not mentioned in polite society.

The guard who was leading the condemned man away when that sound rang out wrinkled his nose in distaste. He had caught a whiff of the odour of flatulence.

1907

The Moasernspitze Expedition

I must make it clear from the very start that it was definitely never my intention, at any time during my travels in Switzerland, to get my neck broken. When I dared to undertake the ascent of the Moasernspitze, I was acting under the influence of a higher power, namely three bottles of wine, and the daughter of the man who kept that lousy inn in Berne where I drank the said wine.

And now, to business. What exactly is the Moasernspitze? Well, since I went climbing on the Moasernspitze, there are no prizes for guessing that it is a mountain: a mountain, moreover, with a 'Spitze', a sharp point, as can easily be deduced from its name. And I hardly need to point out that it is situated in the Alps for no-one, I hope, would imagine that if you are looking for the Himalayas, Switzerland is the place to go.

The Moasernspitze puffs itself proudly up some six hours' journey away from Berne, in the Canton of Berne, and it was of interest for the fact that up to the time of my arrival, no-one had been killed there, for the simple reason that no-one had ever gone clambering about on it.

There are, after all, so many mountains in the vicinity of Berne that this particular dangerous peak had been lost in the multitude and had it not been for the enterprising Bernese innkeeper Herr Grafergeren, no-one to this day would have an inkling of the fact that this is a mountain ideally suited to the various pleasures of mountaineering, as for example neck-breaking, or leg-, spine- and arm-smashing.

The enterprising Herr Grafergeren of Berne saw the advantages of this mountain very well, such as the dangerous valley in which it lay, its sheer peaks, crumbling rock and so on, and conceived the idea of setting up a climber's hut at the foot to which he could lure Englishmen and any others who did not care whether it was Mont Blanc they fell off, or merely the Moasernspitze.

So he established one hut down below and a further four hours' climbing, or rather, crawling on all fours up the mountainside, a second one. By means of donkeys, he stocked both of these huts with drink, wine and spirits, and food and settled down to wait for a first victim, from whom he could get some publicity.

And Fate decreed that I should be the first to fall into his hands. Towards the end of June, then, I was staying at his inn in Berne and was hooked, to use the vulgar parlance, partly by the wine, partly by his daughter Margareta. And Margareta and the wine lured me into the Moasernspitze expedition. I'm not surprised at the wine, but I do wonder at such lack of conscience in a woman.

To Hell with her, that Margareta of Berne! Such are my thoughts today but at the time, inflamed as I was by the wine, I should have volunteered to go to India and climb Mount Everest, let alone the Moasernspitze, which is only three and a half thousand metres high.

It happened this way. Towards evening, on the day of my arrival at Herr Grafergeren's inn, I was sitting with a bottle of wine in front of me and got into a conversation with Margareta.

I didn't know what I was saying. I boasted about the climbs I had made.

'Climbing Mont Blanc,' I said, 'is a piece of cake, Fräulein Margareta. And as for the Grossglockner – a mere pimple! Child's play. A fellow doesn't even feel dizzy.'

At that point, Herr Grafergeren approached.

'Milord,' he said (giving me the title he usually employed, since he assumed from my daredevil tone that I must be an Englishman), 'Milord, I know just the thing for you. A dangerous climb.'

'I never' (I lied to Margareta) 'take on a climb where there's less than a seventy-per-cent chance of a fatal accident. Do you by any chance know, Sir,' (naming a café under the Hradčany in Prague) 'where Mount Nebozízek is?'

'No, Milord, I don't. Is it a dangerous mountain?'

'Out of a hundred people,' I replied coolly, 'hardly five come back from Mount Nebozízek in full working order.'

That impressed even the hard-boiled Grafergeren. 'Milord,' he said, 'I can guarantee you the chance of a fatal accident on the Moasernspitze as well. There are precipices and abysses there two thousand feet deep.'

'That's nothing, Herr Grafergeren. Bring me another bottle of wine, and on the way you can reflect on what I am going to ask you now. Can you guarantee that in the event of an accident I would be smashed completely to smithereens?'

When that worthy man returned with the wine, he answered: 'I can give you my word of honour that you would be reduced to a pulp. As you fell,' he added enticingly, 'you would be dashed at least two hundred times against the sharp projections in the cliffs. And then there's another advantage you should consider carefully: there are terrible raging storms and torrential downpours on the Moasernspitze and I can guarantee that you will be at risk of being washed away by the water and blown into an abyss by the wind.'

'Beginners' stuff, Herr Grafergeren. To a climber of my calibre, that's nothing.'

'Quite, Milord, but just take into account that you would be climbing amongst icefields and that those icefields on the Moasernspitze are anything but innocent little creatures. I can say with confidence that at the very least, eighty per cent of climbers would fall into a crevasse. In short, Milord, a trip up the Moasernspitze would be just what you're looking for. Be so kind as to take into account the fact that this is the only mountain in the area where you can be suddenly overtaken by mist, so that your chances of falling over the edge of a precipice are extremely good, and on top of that, the stone up there is powdery at precisely those places where you are skirting a sheer drop. It really is just made for you.'

'The kind of expedition that would suit you to a tee,' added Margareta.

'Fräulein Grafergeren,' I said, 'would it give you pleasure if I were to climb the Moasernspitze?'

'Yes, Milord,' said Margareta. Go to the Devil, my little Swiss Rose! That's the way I feel today. But on that day, I gave her my hand and said: 'Fräulein Margareta, I will climb the Moasernspitze.'

So I climbed . . .

My guide was called Georg. He was a Catholic as it happened, and he drew my attention with great earnestness to the fact that I could go to confession before we set out. When I declined this kind offer, he asked me to buy him his drink while we were still in Berne. With this request I complied.

He pressed a piece of arsenic upon me, which climbers crunch as if it were sugar.

'The pleasure was all mine,' I said, thanking him heartily.

Georg finished his brandy in businesslike fashion and then asked if he could tie me to him with the safety-rope while we were still in the city. This offer I also declined. And so we set off unattached for Herr Grafergeren's hut, the proprietor himself having meanwhile gone on ahead on his donkey.

'If it should happen that I do not see you again,' Margareta said to me as we parted, 'I'll come to your grave sometimes and say a prayer.' Hearts of gold they have, these Swiss girls.

After an uneventful six-hour walk, we reached Herr Grafergeren's hut, where we stayed overnight and were afforded every comfort by the innkeeper, who proved an excellent host.

In the morning, we set out on the next stage of our journey. As we took our leave, Herr Grafergeren stood there washing his hands and said: 'Milord, is there any message you wish me to convey to your family in the event of an accident?'

'Just tell them,' I replied, 'that I recommend you and the Moasernspitze to all my friends.'

'I'll tell them,' he said in a voice full of eager anticipation, and broke into a yodel.

The higher we went, the more precipitous the path became. Georg tied us together and I can vouch for the fact that he was a good Catholic, because he was praying as he did so.

'What would you do,' I asked him, 'if I were to slip at some point and remain dangling over a precipice, and you were having difficulty holding me in mid-air? Would you wait till help arrived?'

'I'd cut the rope,' said Georg calmly, 'and go and report the accident in Berne. It'd be in the papers that same afternoon and you'd see the stir it would create and the profit that Grafergeren would make from it. All the English would flock here, because your Englishman loves a bit of danger. Old Grafergeren's a shrewd one, eh?'

'A shrewd one indeed!'

I warmed to Georg's frank and open nature. Engaged in an agreeable conversation about fatal accidents to climbers, we ascended higher and higher until we reached the second hut, which stood looking down into an abyss of quite respectable proportions.

We entered the hut and there, while Georg was making goulash from a tin, and preparing the wine, I began to take stock of the situation.

Behind the hut, the thousand-metre-high wall of the Moasernspitze reared itself up like a giant tenement-block, with cliffs all over it, here and there a glitter of ice and the most spine-chilling crevasses.

Hell's teeth! I was supposed to climb that, was I, and get my neck broken somewhere up there? Finally, the scales fell from my eyes. That nice Herr Grafergeren would use my death to publicise the huts he had built and the Moasernspitze which rose above them.

'Georg,' I said to my guide, 'I am not climbing up there.'

Georg took fright. 'That'll never do, Milord,' he said in dismay. 'I'd lose my money.'

'But I've already paid you in advance.'

'I know, Milord, but Herr Grafergeren wouldn't pay me.'

'And what is he supposed to pay you for?'

'For luring you up onto the Moasernspitze.'

'But Georg, suppose I get killed?'

'Then I'd get the same amount and on top of that, it would bring the climbers in, Englishmen, and I'd get more money from them, and more from Herr Grafergeren.'

'And if the Englishmen got killed . . . what then, Georg?'

'Then there'd be all kinds of people climbing the Moasernspitze and I'd be able to put by a nice little pile of francs. So come along, Milord, up we go with a will, eh? If you tumble off, perhaps you'll remain hanging from a cliff as you were afraid you might.'

'Tell you what, Georg, we'll stay here for a couple of days and feed off the provisions. I'll give you twenty francs and then we'll go back, just as if we had climbed the Moasernspitze.'

'I'll be disappointed if it doesn't give old Grafergeren a heart-attack to see me come back from the Moasernspitze safe and sound,' I said to myself, savouring the thought of my revenge.

And so we spent two days in the hut eating and drinking and on the third day we went back down.

Outside Herr Grafergeren's hut, a great surprise awaited us. There were about sixty Englishmen standing there, watching in amazement as we descended. At the head of the group of Englishmen, Herr Grafergeren stood gazing at us goggle-eyed.

'You haven't been killed, then?' he called out to me in consternation.

'As you can see,' I replied in a casual tone, 'I haven't.'

'Sir!' one of the Englishmen shouted in my ear, waving a Berne daily paper under my nose, 'Sir, if you are a gentleman, you will explain this to me . . .'

He handed me the Berne newspaper of the previous day, with this report underlined in blue pencil:

A NEW MOUNTAIN-CLIMB

Our indefatigable Herr Grafergeren has succeeded in discovering a rewarding new climb. This is the Moasernspitze, a mountain in our area which is difficult of access and on which, with typical Swiss attention to detail, he has set up two huts. We regret to have to report that the first expedition to this hitherto unclimbed peak has been accompanied by a disaster. A climber, the first to venture on this ascent, fell yesterday, having failed to pay sufficient attention to the advice of his guide, about whose fate we have as yet no information. It is a very rewarding and dangerous climb which, in view of its many points of interest, will doubtless attract many climbers. An intensive search for the two bodies is in progress. Further particulars from Herr Grafergeren, at his hut at the foot of the Moasernspitze.

'Gentlemen,' I said to the Englishmen, 'this is just a flight of Herr Grafergeren's fancy. The way up is not dangerous in the least, indeed I can state that it is really enjoyable. No more than an afternoon stroll . . .'

'Herr Grafergeren,' said one of the Englishmen, 'we are going back to Berne. This gentleman, as you can see, has not been killed. The ascent is not dangerous: it's a waste of our time. You have been lying to us. Let us go, gentlemen. Good Day!'

'Gentlemen,' cried Herr Grafergeren in piteous tones, 'at least consider the possibility that you might be swept away by an avalanche . . .'

We heard no more, for we had already left his hospitable hut behind us. A stone came flying past us from above and to this day, I do not know whether it had broken off from some cliff or whether it had been hurled down after us by Herr Grafergeren.

As for Fräulein Margareta, I saved her the trip to the cemetery, where she had intended to dedicate a prayer to me.

A heart of gold, that's me . . .

1907

The Betyár's Tale

Kigyó and Teher were lying on the moss under the leafy branches of an oak-tree and cursing the world in general and the local Mayor in particular.

The two of them, young fellows of about thirty, belonged to that caste in Magyar society which rejoices in the resounding title of *betyár*, which denotes a herdsman or a good-for-nothing, an artful dodger in general.

Kigyó and Teher were swineherds in the first place and good-for-nothings and artful dodgers in the second; betyárs of the first rank, the kind that can be parted from their short pipes only when they have been up to some mischief and have landed themselves in jail, where they also have to exchange their breeches and jackets for the grey garb of the convict.

Just now, they were having a good curse, an activity that occupies at least a third of the lives of this rare breed of men.

Kigyó had just finished cursing the Mayor's grandfather when Teher remembered that he hadn't cursed the Mayor's aunt.

Whereupon Kigyó in his turn consigned the Mayor's aunt's mother to the nether regions but then, so that everyone should be remembered in proper form, they took cognisance of the fact that none of the Mayor's relatives was alive and so Kigyó pronounced solemnly: '*Mindt öröké, amen*' (For ever and ever, Amen).

All around them, in the oak-grove, the communal herd of the village of Talom was dotted about, grazing, squealing and grunting. Some were rootling in the ground for acorns and here and there a piglet scampered and pigs wallowed in the lazily flowing stream, revelling in the chance to cool their thick skins in the black mud after they had been baked in the blazing heat of the sunny day.

All the colours of the porcine rainbow were represented here, from the pink tints of the smooth-skinned breeds to the curly-haired black ones. Pigs, boars, sows and piglets; boars that grunted angrily as they thrust the others away with their tusks, fat sows that grunted lovingly as, at every time of asking, they satisfied the demands of greedily sucking piglets.

And around them ran two dogs of the breed that is used for watching over these useful animals and originated in the distant past from a cross between dogs and wolves.

With their running and barking and baring of teeth, they kept the whole great herd in order, so that the two herdsmen could lie under their tree in peace without needing to reach for the long whips they had left lying about on the moss.

Teher did nevertheless pick up his whip on one occasion, when one of the Mayor's little pigs ran by. He raised the whip and brought it down again across its back, so that it ran off squealing to look for acorns somewhere else.

Having thus vented his spleen on the Mayor's property, Teher made himself comfortable in the moss once again, emitted a puff of smoke from his lips and as he watched it slowly drifting away on the windless air, pronounced magisterially: 'And what sort of man is the Mayor in any case? A drunk, no better than a drunk! And a man like that is trying to stop me marrying Františka Homlóková!'

Kigyó, his partner, looked solemn and said: 'Tell me the story again.'

'Well, it was this way. Františka and I have been going together for two years. I go and visit them every so often. As you know, I show great respect to Homlók's pigs and guide them to all the best spots.

'Old Homlók didn't raise any objection. He always said: "All right, lad, so you're just a betyár: so what? I was just a betyár once. But I knew what was what. I used to fatten up the animals they gave me as payment and sell them at a profit. My pigs sold well. In the capital they still remember Homlók's pigs to this day. Now and then I would steal one and put it down to bears and wolves. With the money I got for them, I would buy young pigs and bring them on and sell them again for a good price. I sweated for twenty years and finally I'd amassed such a pile that Birka the farmer let his daughter marry a betyár. So why shouldn't I let my daughter marry you? Just carry on the good work."

'So it was all going swimmingly. Till the day before yesterday when, after we had driven the herd home and you'd gone off for a glass of wine, I went as usual to visit the Homlóks.

'There in the parlour sat old Homlók and opposite him, Mayor Nárva.

'They were so deep in conversation that they didn't see me. I went over to the fireplace in the corner, sat down and listened.

'"My son Ferencz," said the Mayor, "is sweet on your Františka."'

'"There's no future in that, friend," replied Homlók, "Because I've already . . ."'

'"They say, Homlók, that you're going to let your daughter marry some layabout of a betyár."'

'I was about to jump up, but then I thought: "Let's see what old Homlók will answer to that."'

'So I listen and I hear: "Birka let his daughter marry some layabout of a betyár, Mayor; me, in fact."'

'The Mayor was stopped in his tracks. "You weren't any ordinary betyár. But Teher, well, that's another kettle of fish. Nobody knows whose son he is. A gypsy's, they say. His mother wasn't respectable; she was in service in a nobleman's house. She died as she lived: drank till she'd drunk herself to death . . ."'

'"Mayor," I heard Homlók say, "let's let the dead lie quiet in their graves. You ruined a woman once, in Farád. The child died and you couldn't make an honest woman of the girl from Farád because you were already married when it happened. We all of us like a little drink and it was God who made the wine but the way you drink is just not Christian."'

'"So you're going to let that good-for-nothing Teher have your daughter?"'

'"I reckon so."'

'"Do you know that Teher's a thief? It's not all that long since a sow went missing . . ."'

'"I know, I've been a betyár myself."'

'"And I'm sure you know that Teher is the village council's swineherd and I can have him thrown out of his job?"'

'"I know that too, but a betyár can always get by."'

'So the Mayor went off in a huff and when he had gone I came out of the corner and said: "Homlók, I heard all that. – You're going to let me have Františka, then?"'

'"Yes I am," answered Homlók, "but only after you've taken revenge on the Mayor: for yourself, for me and for the whole race of betyárs." What do you think of that, Kigyó?'

'You could set fire to his farm,' suggested Kigyó, 'lie in wait for him and stick him with a knife good and proper.'

Teher shook his head. 'Can't do that . . . it would be a sin,' he said, calmly puffing out a wreath of smoke, and as he lay there, he began to whistle and his whistling eventually turned into song.

He sang one of those betyár songs about a tavern out in the depths of the *puszta* and about a woman not quite past her youth who kept the tavern and had a pretty niece. And a betyár fell in love with the niece and she took the girl far out into the *puszta* in the winter-time and left her there to die, for she grudged her the handsome betyár.

And when he heard this, he rode to the tavern and thrust a dagger into the tavern-keeper's heart.

Kigyó joined in and finished with a crack of his whip.

The shadows of the trees in the oak-grove were lengthening. The wood was growing dark with the dusk of evening. It was time now to drive the herd home and they whistled to the dogs, got up and shouted: 'Hey, hey! Hoy, hoy!'

A lively movement arose among the animals. Those that were rolling about in the grass and the mud got up and joined the others.

The dogs ran round them and made them collect together in a group.

'Hoy, hoy!' The herdsmen cracked their whips, sending an echo like a gun-shot through the forest: 'Bang!'

And slowly, the herd got under way.

It was one of Mayor Nárva's unlovely characteristics that he would stay outside the door of a room he had just left to hear whether anyone said anything about him. He hung about this time as well, after he had parted from Homlók, and heard, to his astonishment, the voices of Teher speaking and the old man answering: 'I'll give you Františka, but only after you've taken revenge on the Mayor: for yourself, for me and for the whole race of betyárs.'

Half dead with fright, he barely managed to get home – and then he shut himself away in his parlour. He was so scared he forgot about smoking and did not once dip into his wine-jug. He would not reply to anyone's questions and went to bed, but could not get to sleep.

His fear of Teher's revenge renewed in his mind the memory of old tales about the betyárs of the Hungarian *puszta* who, in olden days, had stuck the Lord of the Manor on a spit and roasted him.

Over and over again, his thoughts turned to the savagery of those people. Next day, he pulled himself together and went to see the village notary and ask his advice.

The notary, a very young person who had only recently completed his studies in the city and who was now thrust straight out from the urban bustle, performing the monotonous duties of his office here, received the frightened Mayor most amiably.

He kept a good slivovic which he used to take the edge off his village solitude and after the fifth glass, the wretched Mayor had come to himself a little and began to explain the purpose of his visit.

'I'm very unhappy, Your Worship, because I could wake up tomorrow and find my throat cut.'

'Well, in that case,' was the smiling observation of the notary, 'you wouldn't wake up.'

'There's more than one way, Your Worship, that I could be killed. I could be strangled, drowned, hung, shot or disembowelled. It's horrible!'

The Mayor wiped the sweat from his brow with his shirt-sleeve, which did duty for him as a handkerchief.

'This is wild talk, my friend.'

'Now, Your Worship, you see me sitting here in front of you alive and in an hour's time, maybe, someone will find my dead body. God knows what is going to happen to me.'

'But who is it, my friend?'

'The betyár, Your Worship.'

The notary frowned. He was well aware that these people were not to be trifled with.

'And he threatened you?'

'Oh no, Teher hasn't threatened me personally up to now.'

And the Mayor told the story of his visit to Homlók.

'He'll revenge himself on me, I know for certain he will. And a betyár's revenge is a terrible thing. Oh, why did my Ferencz send me to Homlók?' lamented the Mayor. 'I can see that my days are numbered.'

The notary scratched his head in perplexity. 'What about locking Teher up?'

'God forbid, Your Worship; that would only end in a nasty death.'

'Suppose I go and talk to him?'

'I'll give the priest two gulden to pray for you while you're there.'

In spite of the seriousness of the situation, the notary had to smile. 'I doubt whether he'll touch me. I'll go straight away. Where have they got the herd?'

'In Mérges* Valley.'

* 'Poison' (J. H.)

The notary set off on the instant, with the thanks of the Mayor in his ears.

On leaving the village, he climbed a little hill. Then he followed the path down to the oak-grove and the nearer he came to Mérges Valley, the more his courage ebbed. The brisk pace changed into a leisurely stroll. He lit a cigarette and proceeded slowly in the direction from which the barking of dogs and the grunting of pigs could be heard.

Today, as yesterday, Kigyó and Teher were lying in the shade of the oak-tree. Kigyó was snoring, stretched comfortably out on the loose earth, and Teher was smoking his pipe as he pondered his revenge.

Such was their disposition when the notary came upon them, and stood irresolutely under the oak-tree.

Teher prodded Kigyó and they both sat up.

'Good Day,' the notary greeted them, when he had approached as far as their outstretched feet.

'Good Day,' they answered casually.

Ill at ease in this atmosphere, the young notary began a conversation: 'You've found a nice place to lie in, I see.'

The dogs were leaping round him like mad things. Kigyó drove them off with his whip and lay down on the ground again.

'Not so terribly hot today,' the notary went on.

'You're right there,' said Teher. 'It isn't all that hot.'

The notary plucked up courage. 'I've come, friends, on the Mayor's behalf.'

Teher didn't say a word. Reassured by this, the community notary went on: 'The Mayor has found out by chance that his conversation with Homlók has been misunderstood. I've come to tell you in his name that when he said what he said it was just a sudden burst of irritation . . . under the influence, so to speak.'

'So that old soak's afraid of me, is he?' asked the young betyár, jumping up.

The question was put so directly that the notary could not but answer: 'Yes.'

'That's all right, then.'

'What am I to tell the Mayor?'

'Why, that everything's all right.' Teher's eyes flashed as he lay down under the tree again.

The notary went away reassured, but when he later reported the result of his mission to the Mayor, Nárva shook with despair on his bench. 'When a betyár says that everything's fine, it means he's going to do what he's decided to do. Nothing can save me, Your Worship.'

When Teher told Homlók about the notary's visit that evening, old Homlók said calmly: 'But that doesn't mean you're not to take your revenge, my boy.'

'I'll get my revenge, Homlók,' said the betyár.

Summer went by, autumn passed, winter arrived and the whole countryside round about was covered in snow. In his little cottage on the edge of the village, Teher brooded on his revenge. Outside, the frost was glittering everywhere, but the fire of vengeance burned bright in Teher's heart. It warmed him as much as if he had put any number of logs in the fire that crackled in his hearth.

The Mayor meanwhile was petrified with fear. He felt like a condemned man who does not know when the executioner will come for him. If you slander a betyár, you can expect no mercy from him.

One winter's day, the Mayor went into town to make his will. He had put it off for a long time, but now at last . . .

And at the same moment as he arrived in the town, Teher entered it from the other side. During those days, he had not let the Mayor out of his sight.

Shrovetide was approaching. He needed to take his revenge and then get married. What form his revenge would take, he did not know, but he had sworn that it would be something brutal.

He missed the Mayor in town. In his annoyance, he went off to a tavern and did not leave it till evening, not long after the Mayor had set off for home.

Nárva had changed his mind about making his will, for no sooner had he entered the town than the warmth that emanated from a certain tavern proved so irresistible that he had gone in to warm up his frozen bones with a jar of wine. But once inside the tavern, he didn't stop at just one jug. He drank till evening and then emerged as night was falling over the snow-covered countryside.

Over towards the east, where his home village lay, it was already growing dark. The winter's night was coming steadily closer and closer from that side, while from the west a snowstorm was sweeping eastwards.

The befuddled Mayor was in no fit state to find his way. The wine and the snow weighed his feet down.

His heavy fur coat became heavier still as the snow fell without interruption.

It settled on his moustache, melting in his warm breath and freezing into icicles under the lash of the freezing wind.

All around, there was nothing but snow and more snow, growing deeper and deeper and making it so very hard to walk.

His feet slithered in the soft snow and suddenly, he had fallen.

He tried to get up and managed to do so, but there was a sudden gust of wind and it was as if, from somewhere out there, a terrible fatigue had come upon him. Nárva fell face down into a pile of drifted snow.

The snow on his boots melted and as with his moustache, a skin of ice wrapped itself round his kneecaps.

He was unable to get up. He became dimly aware that he was freezing to death. Suddenly, it seemed to him that it was not winter; it was spring and he had lain down in the warmth of the sun on the edge of a wood . . .

And then someone was shaking him and lifting him and holding him to stop him falling. 'Come on, stir yourself, you old drunkard!'

'Leave me in peace,' grunted the Mayor, making an attempt to lie down in the snow again.

'I ought to leave you here to freeze,' growled a familiar voice, 'but I'm not going to.'

Strong hands grasped the Mayor under the armpits; the man was marching him off to his village.

He heard the cursing of whoever was carrying him and then fell asleep . . . He didn't wake up till he was home, wrapped up in his feather-bed.

'What happened?' he asked in astonishment.

'You lay down in the snow. Teher found you and brought you home,' replied his son Ferencz, putting a bottle of slivovic to his lips.

When the young betyár came back from the Mayor's house and told Homlók what had happened, old Homlók, the former betyár, could not hold back the tears.

'You waited long enough for your revenge,' he said, 'and it came. You youngsters are better men than us old ones. In your place, I would have left him lying there . . . But for all that, you're not getting Františka . . .'

And that is the betyár's tale.

And I swear that all the betyárs, the swineherds of the Badačon heights, be they *kondás* or *kanasz*,* behave in just this way.

1907

---

* Magyar words, both meaning 'swineherd'.

Father Ondřej's Sin

Father Ondřej was now into his eighteenth year in Purgatory and he still didn't know why. His case had still not reached the stage of final sentence, even though the pressure of souls coming into Purgatory had eased in the last year or two. The majority of souls nowadays just made a temporary halt here and were then led off, amid gnashing of teeth, to Hell. Occasionally, he would pluck up the courage to ask one of the Angel Guards: 'Why are you keeping me here, gentlemen?'

They would shrug their wings and say: 'Your case has still not been decided, Reverend Sir.'

These words always made him feel uneasy as only a soul in Purgatory can feel uneasy, for he was not conscious of having committed any sin. He was a textbook example of the venerable priest. During his time on earth, he had fitted the description in every particular: the long white hair, the quavering old-man's voice, the moral purity, First Class.

And here he was, still held in investigative detention in Purgatory.

Of late, he had enjoyed the company of a certain chaplain, who could look forward to a ten-thousand-year stretch. At the Jubilee Exhibition, the poor devil had spent a quarter of an hour watching the people tobogganing down a chute, and then had had a stroke on the way home.

'Real Brussels lace, Father,' the wretched chaplain would say to Father Ondřej, whose pure soul could not grasp the difference between an ordinary petticoat and a lace one.

And the angels flew quietly around him. They felt sorry for him and sang him lovely songs to words taken from the Holy Fathers. And they said: 'Send in a petition, Father.'

And he submitted a petition in writing:

To the Most Honourable Court of Last Judgment:

The soul undersigned hereby begs to submit his most humble petition for release from Purgatory, advancing as justification for his respectful request the following grounds:

A. The undersigned can find nothing in his conscience to count against him.

B. He has been thoroughly purified, as can be attested by local magistrate Paluška, at present located in cauldron 253 in the Temperate Purgatorial Zone, where the ventilators are.

C. This same statement, that he is purified and without blemish, can be verified by Police Sergeant Josef Loukota, currently resident, in a state of beatitude, in Heaven, near turnstile No. 5.

D. The undersigned discovered a miraculous spring and dispensed water from it to orphanages and houses of correction, free of charge.

E. He distinguished himself as a student, as will be confirmed by Alexius, the Headmaster of his Grammar School, now attached to the Angel Grammar School Guard Unit in Purgatory.

F. The undersigned has a particularly good grasp of Latin, Greek, Hebrew and Aramaic.

G. The undersigned has never been troubled by any doubt on any subject.

On the above grounds, he requests his release from Purgatory and undertakes, should his most respectful request be acceded to, to bend his every effort to ensuring that he proves himself worthy of that trust.

This petition was sent back. 'The rubric's missing,' said the angel who brought it. This angel had worked, during his earthly life, as an official in a government department.

So Father Ondřej wrote on the reverse side: 'Soul Father Ondřej requests his release from Purgatory under headings A,B,C,D,E,F, and G.'

On the anniversary of his death – they're usually no quicker in giving their kind attention to a petition on earth, either – he received a reply:

Honoured Sir,

We take the liberty of informing you that the Court of Last Judgment will not be sitting in the foreseeable future. We have accordingly directed your petition to the High Court of Purgatory, with the request that it should receive the most urgent consideration and that you should be brought before the Regular Purgatorial Sessions for the examination of your sin.

On behalf of the Preliminary Examining Committee of the Court of Last Judgment,

(Signed) Gabriel

And the years flowed quietly by, to the accompaniment of the groaning of souls under purification and the touching lullabies of the angels as they rocked the cradles of the unbaptised.

At last, Father Ondřej received a summons to present himself before the Sacred Senate.

The Senate was already assembled in the pergola of the Lower Court of Purgatory, visible only to the Angel Guards who had brought in the accused. The book of Father Ondřej's life hovered in mid-air, the pages turned by an invisible hand.

'Father Ondřej,' said a voice, 'you see here the book of your life. It is clean, except for one page. I charge you now to answer truthfully to this question: did you have a brother in Australia?'

'I did, My Lords of the Senate.'

'We ask you further: did you write to your brother in Australia?'

'Yes, My Lords; to Sydney, in the year 1882.'

The book was closed and a deep voice rang out, a voice that, to all appearances, belonged to the President of the Sacred Senate: 'Have you studied thoroughly all the books written by Saint Augustine, the Teacher of the Church?'

'I have.'

And now, a rustling of wings was heard. The court was retiring to consider its verdict. A renewed rustle of wings, and a voice from above cried out:

'Father Ondřej is sentenced to fifteen thousand years of enforced confinement in Purgatory, inclusive of twenty-two years of investigative detention. The reasons for this decision are as follows:

'In his book *De Retractione, vel Librorum Recensione*, Augustine, the Teacher of the Church, declared belief in the existence of the antipodes to be a heresy (see page 213). Since Australia is part of the antipodes, belief in the existence of Australia constitutes the sin of blasphemy, committed and confirmed by Father Ondřej by the act of sending a letter to his brother in the antipodes, to wit in Sydney, Australia. The purified state of the accused and his full and frank confession constitute extenuating circumstances.'

'Don't cry,' the angels said consolingly to the condemned man. 'You could have had something like that happen to you in any court on earth.'

1908

Here Today, Gone Tomorrow

It was already a good five o'clock in the afternoon when Juraj Vručić finally succeeded after great efforts in extricating himself from the scrub down by the River Dráva; the prickly juniper, long grass and young oaks with which the low ground by the river is overgrown.

He found himself on a better track, a sandy one, beaten flat by carts and trampled down by the hooves of cattle. Here, he also had a better view of his surroundings. The sandy track wound its way between low willow-trees which formed a vista down which he could see the outlines of a village: little white houses, the greenery of the fruit-trees, the red-coloured tower of a little church and in front of the village, fields of maize swaying in the wind.

Juraj Vručić drew a deep breath and sat down in the grass for a while. He looked at the village and smiled contentedly when he saw the blue hills rising in the distance behind it. It was from the vineyards up there that the red wine had come he had drunk that morning in Varaždín.

'That was a wine, that was! You drink one litre and you feel it pushing down into your legs. Then you drink a second and you feel it warming you up and merry thoughts come rising up out of your legs into your head. You drink the third, and you begin to sing; why, you even make up songs of your own. When you're on number four, every vein in your body begins to tremble and you feel like taking a header. Then you go outside and what you intend to do is drive home to Sudovčina, but you take a wrong turning and you find yourself on the road to Ormoz, heading for Styria. Then suddenly, you have a good idea: you're on a wrong track; you have to go by Štefanec, Semovec, Zamxak, Ebanovec and then on home to Sudovčina. You turn back to Varaždín, go round the castle, past the barracks and look for the road to Štefanec. You ask the way, laugh, sway from side to side, the people you ask laugh as well and finally you're somewhere or other, driving down towards the River Dráva. There are trails leading in all directions. There's a track somewhere that leads headlong down to the river. And that damned wine inside you seems to want to jump. You find yourself stumbling and there you are with your hands in the juniper bushes and you're getting pricked. And no sooner have you stood up than you've got your arms round a little oak tree or you're falling about in the brambles. But here you are on a good road at last, thank God! and you can see the village!'

Juraj Vručić said all that to himself as he sat at the crossroads. He took one more look at the village and then went on, gazing up at the blue sky: 'Today, friends, Juraj Vručić will be late home from market. In the morning, I hitched up the horses and drove to Varaždín. Well, it was a horse and a mare. There was a foal trotting alongside the mare. A lovely foal! I said to my farm-hand: "Ride quickly, lad, so that we can get to Varaždín and get a good price for the foal." So we ride and we sell the foal for sixty gulden. I send the farm-hand home and I go and have a little drink.'

Juraj Vručić stopped talking to the sky and turned to a bushy alder-tree. 'A beautiful foal, that was! Not like my neighbour's. That one ran itself into a post, poor thing, and ripped its stomach open. The doctor sewed it together again but it wasn't up to much . . . Well, praise be to my patron saint, here I am at last . . . And what a lot of pretty girls I saw at the market . . . and what a good market it was! I'll get up now and go on.'

Vručić clambered laboriously to his feet, crossed himself and felt carefully at his leather satchel.

'The money's still there,' he said, laughing, and walked slowly along the sandy track.

At six o'clock, he was in Štefanec. He might have got there earlier, but he had fallen into the maize as he was looking to see how big the cobs were. And he had delayed himself further by considering, as he lay there in the maize-field, which of the girls he would have chosen if he hadn't been married; which, that is, of the girls he had seen at the market. At last, he had got up and with a mumbled: 'Whatever you say, my dear,' proceeded into Štefanec.

He went slowly through the village until he got to the very end, where he stopped, his attention having been caught by a straw sign made of maize-stalks that hung over the gate of a house.

It wasn't the ordinary sign you see hanging outside other taverns, or farmsteads where you can get the farmer to draw you a glass of wine. This was a gigantic sign. It hung swaying on a bar, rustling in the breeze, and the longer Juraj Vručić looked at that sign, the keener his thirst became. He knew this place. Oh yes! There over the door was the legend: 'The Jolly Anthony'. Any number of times he had stopped here, but now he saw something else written above the name of the establishment that he had never noticed before.

He took a few steps back, so that he could see it better, and read:

> Here today, gone tomorrow,
> Holy writ decrees our sorrow;
> Where were you? the Lord would ask
> If you'd not drunk from Tony's cask.

'Here today, gone tomorrow,' Vručić said to himself. 'That's the sacred truth. Where were you? Strange, God would ask where you'd been . . . Oh, I see, it says: Where were you, the Lord would ask, if you'd not drunk from Tony's cask? There's a new thought: the Lord God himself would ask: "Why didn't you have a drink at Tony's place?" Sacred truth, that. It's a sin to pass by the Jolly Anthony and not have even a half litre of wine. Here today, gone tomorrow, and our Heavenly Father would be angry with us.'

Vručić fell silent and then, taking no notice of the crowd of village children standing around him, declared in a resolute voice: 'Juraj Vručić, you're going in for a half litre of wine!'

He went into the inn and in less than a quarter of an hour from the time of his arrival, he had an empty half-litre bottle standing in front of him.

'We're here today, and we're gone tomorrow,' Vručić pronounced. 'Landlord, another half-litre. We don't want our Heavenly Father to be angry with us. That's well said, what you've got written over your door.'

'And that really is a good interpretation of mine,' he thought, as he dealt with the second half-litre. 'Anyone who doesn't drink wine as good as this is guilty of a terrible sin. Our district priest now, he does say that if you drink, you give your soul to the Devil; but here, it says: "Where were you, the Lord would ask if you'd not drunk from Tony's cask." Here, you're a sinner if you don't drink. And why should I be a sinner, I, Juraj Vručić, with money to spare now that I've sold my foal for a good price? All right then, I'll have a full litre. Here today, gone tomorrow . . .'

It was eight o'clock in the evening when Vručić started out on his homeward way again. He took one more look at the inscription over the door, gave a grunt of approval as he did so and then set course with tottering steps for Semovec. Night had begun to fall; the herds were coming home from pasture, all around there was the tinkling of cow-bells, the stamping of hooves and the cracking of whips. The mounted herdsmen, riding along on their horses, shouted at Vručić, who still kept on grunting: 'Here today, gone tomorrow.'

He ploughed straight ahead and rested occasionally, here on a pile of gravel with which he had collided, there in a ditch into which he had fallen in getting out of the way of the herds and the horses.

Finally, he lost his way. Unbeknown to him, he had turned off the main road on to another track which led, through meadows that stretched out between the bushes, towards the Dráva and split into a countless multitude of paths, reappearing when the latter merged into one single stream of white sand and finally vanishing, in the darkness of evening, into the mist that was rolling across meadows and bushes.

Oblivious of all this, he walked. On and on he walked, forcing his way forwards with the bushes tearing at his clothes.

In the quiet of that evening down by the River Dráva, there rang out from his lips, to an unknown melody, the words: 'Here today, gone tomorrow, Holy Writ decrees our sorrow . . .'

Close at hand, the darkness resounded with a droning sound, the sound a river makes as it roars and foams.

Without knowing it, Juraj Vručić was standing at that moment on the bank of the River Dráva, on one of those high banks which from year to year are being constantly broadened and hollowed out and crumble by day and by night . . .

'Here today, gone tomorrow,' the words rang out.

Juraj Vručić had reached the very edge. He burst into song once more. 'Here today,' resounded from the bank and 'gone tomorrow' echoed up from below and was drowned in the droning of the river.

Juraj Vručić was swept away by the wild current of the Dráva out of which, at spots like that, not even a good swimmer could have swum to safety.

Here today, gone tomorrow!

(?) before 1910

Election Day With the Young Czech Party in the Malá Strana

I

At three o'clock in the afternoon, they knew in the editorial office of *The Day* that the victory of Dr Vilém Funk was a certainty and they were discussing whether they should print a special edition in which it would be announced that the Young Czechs had succeeded in winning by a gigantic majority in the Malá Strana.

The editorial committee resolved to bring out the special edition and a member of the editorial staff was given the job of writing an enthusiastic article on the outcome of the election.

At a quarter past three, the *National* already had an article set up for the evening edition under the heading: 'Victory Assured for Dr Funk'.

And then at half past three, in the offices of the Young Czech weekly *The People*, Miss Süssová, the 'Young Czech Maid of Orleans', was given the proofs of her own article for the special edition of *The People* which was to proclaim the complete victory of Dr Funk.

She had written that article out of a heart brimming over with political fervour. In ringing tones, the Maid of Orleans declared:

> The fact that Dr Funk has triumphed in today's election by such a splendid majority is one for which we have to thank those fearless warriors who, undeterred by the fury of the demagogues, voted unanimously for Dr Funk as a man most thoroughly acquainted with conditions in the Malá Strana, an exceptionally level-headed politician, a master of economic management and a sincere friend of the inhabitants of our lovely Malá Strana and of Hradčany. This level-headed politician was opposed by Dr Šviha who, on being informed that he had lost by such an overwhelming majority, burst into tears. And it is in tears that National Social politics must end, whereas our proud and victorious Young Czech banner stands unfurled over Royal Hradčany. Not since the time of the coronation of Ferdinand the Goodhearted has the Malá Strana witnessed scenes of rapture to match

those that occurred when it became known that Dr Funk had been victorious. Many ladies threw flowers into Dr Funk's conveyance; the horses were unharnessed and the carriage was drawn by exulting crowds up to the Radetzky Monument, where Dr Funk made a speech about the progress of the Young Czech Idea. Old and young embraced each other . . .

It was a really lovely article, beautiful and strong, like the convictions of Miss Süssová herself who, as is well-known, comes of a long line of Young Czechs. Even before the birth of Christ, they say, her ancestors were Young Czechs. Yes, this was an article full of passion and unshakeable faith; the same faith that moved the French Maid of Orleans to believe that it was really she who was burning the English, not the English who were burning her.

'This special edition of *The People*,' she said prophetically in the printing-room, 'will be an historical document one day.' Then she went off to the Young Czech campaign office to make sure that they had delivered the roses that were to be thrown by Young Czech ladies – for a fee of one crown per lady – into Dr Funk's carriage.

You wouldn't believe the amount of work it takes before they're all dressed and fitted out, and then the effort involved in keeping a sharp look-out to ensure that they don't wander off in those dresses. There's just as much positive politics in that as there is in getting yourself pulled around in a carriage by public servants. When you enter positive politics, you're in the business of buying in enthusiastic support. Some, like the Roman Caesars, get to be pulled along in their carriages because people are afraid of losing their heads. The public servants who were pulling Dr Funk's carriage at this by-election were not in fear for their necks; they were pulling him down Neruda Street for six crowns a man. For twelve, they'd have pulled him to Břevnov and for fifty, as far as Slaný.

At four o'clock, a postcard was delivered to the Young Czech Election Headquarters, bearing a portrait of Dr Funk and the inscription: 'Imperial Deputy Dr Funk, elected for the Fifth Electoral District, 24th June, 1909'.

The man who had brought the postcard then went off to vote. And of course, he voted for Dr Funk.

II

All was hustle and bustle meanwhile at the Young Czech Election Headquarters. This was the point at which the clans gathered when, exercising their right of universal suffrage, they turned up for a free drink. It was all done very discreetly. A thousand glasses appeared on the table and after a while, those glasses were empty. Another four hundred appeared and met the same fate; beer is there to be drunk, just as a ballot-paper is there to be handed, not to the conductor in a tram, but to the official in charge of the polling-station.

And then, why shouldn't a Social Democrat make himself a crown or two when the struggle for social welfare is, after all, Social Democrat policy?

And it was in pursuit of their social interest that they made their way hence with somewhat uncertain steps, to the polling-station.

There was a cloakroom at the back where coats were lent out and hats exchanged, just as your Social Democrat exchanges convictions.

Dr Funk referred to them as his 'valued friends'.

Ah, what a beautiful harmony! And just as, in church, the believer breathes in the intoxicating odour of incense, so here, the air was redolent of the scent of beer and slivovic.

And then a dish of minced beef appeared on the table, emitting a smell that just *made* you go and vote Young Czech.

There were many who came here as Social Democrats. They would drink one beer, a second and then a third, acquire a ballot-paper with Dr Funk's name on it, knock back a slivovic for good measure, and go off to vote.

Dr Vilém Funk! The name that was to them as a spring of water to a thirsty man!

What's that point of having the right to vote if you can't get something out of it?

For extreme contingencies, the municipal drunk-carts were held in readiness, for it is the duty of the City Fathers to lend the voter their support.

They were called upon in only two cases. These two voters, drunk on beer and political fervour, had not managed to make it as far as the polling-station. At the police-station, they were found to be carrying ballot-papers in the name of the Young Czech candidate in their hands and badges supporting the Social Democrats on their coats. A stalwart citizen from Nový Svět in Hradčany was at the centre of a moving scene. Back at the Young Czech Headquarters, he had drunk twelve glasses, and yet he had still managed to cast his vote. But when he emerged onto the steps outside the polling-station, he removed his boots and fell asleep. There was a similarity here to the case of the Athenian runner who carried his message on foot from Sparta to Athens and then, having delivered it, fell to the ground and expired. Heroic feats of this magnitude are few and far between in the annals of History.

'Victory is assured,' said the Young Czech campaign-manager at Election Headquarters. 'Drink up, friends, and when the election's over, there'll be a double ration of beer for you.'

III

At the Young Czech Club, meanwhile, they were getting the carriage ready. 'Don't pull the reins too tight: we want to be able to get the horses out straight away.' After an embarrassing episode with the public servants, they had hired people who were not wearing official caps. Young ones and old ones.

These people were on the point of graduating: passing their graduation-exam in the science of unharnessing the horses from Dr Funk's carriage; taking their Final Examination in the art of giving three cheers.

It was in the cellar that this latter activity was going on: the Viva, in fact. 'Three cheers for our beloved deputy Dr Funk!' 'Hip, hip, Hooray!'

Meanwhile, in a special location, they were rehearsing the musicians hired by the Young Czech Election Committee to fall in, as soon as the great and certain victory of Dr Funk had been proclaimed, behind the carriage, which would be being drawn along by old and young folk alike, and play. Play a victory march, that is. For the most part, they had had to go and vote for Dr Funk before the rehearsal, and that was because it was already down in black and white in *The People* that: 'from the mature electorate, the Young Czech officials on the spot swiftly selected a band, to provide an accompaniment for the cheering crowds.'

The carriage-horses got beer as well. It's a pity, by the way, that real animals don't vote Young Czech. Every horse in Prague would vote then.

'Good God! Look at the way you're taking out that horse, you clumsy oaf! Grab hold of the shaft at the front! Come on, man, put some heart into it! If you're going to rock the carriage about like that, you at the back, we'll have wasted six crowns on you! You've got to really *feel* that jubilation! And you've got to shout in unison. Come on lads, let's have a bit more fire!'

And it wasn't just six-crown-a-time youngsters they had there. A number of older, mustachioed men at eight crowns each were practising as well, for in its report, already set up for the printer, *The Day* had written:

> And with one accord, old and young alike rushed to the coach, cheering with all their might, and unharnessed the horses. The joy that burst out at that moment is beyond description. Ladies threw roses into the coach; the people sang: 'Where my home is'. It was an unforgettable moment. The truth had prevailed. And behind those fervent crowds, the vanquished demagogues stood gnashing their teeth.

IV

At four o'clock, word spread that the voters of Vršovice had not come to Dr Funk's aid. The Young Czechs from Michle had gone missing as well. The people who sleep in the brickyards at Dejvice and in the quarries of Strahov had not turned up to vote for Dr Funk because the police had moved them on the previous night. But it would not do to say that the police were responsible for Dr Funk's defeat.

Dr Funk was assured of victory. The Young Czech cause was on the march. Special editions of *The Day* and *The People* had been set up.

And yet, 35,000 crowns had gone down the drain!

Dr Funk was already sitting in his carriage. All they had to do was set the horses in motion, drive out into the street and there were the six- and eight-crowners waiting to unharness the horses.

And it had all been for nothing!

Dr Šviha won. Dr Funk never had the horses taken out of his carriage.

And so the Young Czech election campaign was a fiasco.

But the Young Czech Maid of Orleans has not given up the struggle.

She is writing a long article for *The People* under the heading: 'A Moral Victory'.

1909

An Investigative Expedition

Not long before the Monarch was due to make a tour of the occupied territories, Officer Vojović of the Political Section of the Bosnian Provincial Police Department was sent to spy out the attitude of the Mayor of Šibak, a town on the route from Bosenský Brod to Mostar, who was thought to be opposed to the government.

Having dressed himself as a peasant, Vojović enquired where Mayor Božetic was in the habit of drinking his wine, and made his way there.

He seated himself opposite Božetic and when he had drunk a half-litre of wine, he started a conversation by asking the Mayor for a little tobacco.

'They say that the Emperor Franz Joseph will be travelling to Hercegovina,' he said cautiously.

'That's right,' said Mayor Božetic, 'Bey Ismailic was talking about it when we were having coffee at Govariv, the Turk's place.'

'God keep him safe and well,' said Vojović.

'God preserve him,' observed Božetic, 'they say he's gone grey now, our Tsar.'

'True, he's gone grey,' said Vojović. 'Before the war we had . . . why, we still have brothers in Serbia.'

'Oh no, you're wrong there. I haven't got any brothers in Serbia. Jovanović, the saddler in Šibak: he's the one who's got brothers in Serbia. One of them's in Kragujevac; he's a saddler as well. And the other's in Belgrade, he makes sweets.'

Vojović bit his lip. 'No, I meant blood-brothers, men of a common tongue . . .'

Božetic waved a hand: 'No, I tell you again, I haven't a single brother in the whole kingdom of Serbia. All I've got over there is a cousin on my aunt-in-law's side. Sáva Miletić, he's called, a lad with a squint in one eye who works in a hotel in Belgrade that's run by a German.'

Vojović was silent for a while. 'But,' he said, 'they do say that we in Bosnia and Hercegovina are one heart, one soul and one tongue with the Serbs.'

'What do you mean, one tongue?' replied Božetic. 'The Serbs don't say "čo" and "ča", but "šta" or "što" and then instead of "d'", they have "dz". Stupid idiot! Our brothers are the Germans. They've built us a railway and brought in goats.'

Vojović refused to give up hope. 'They've brought in taxes as well.'

'Taxes? So what, you thick-head? I'm glad to pay them, as long as I can live under an efficient administration,' said Božetic. 'And if the time comes that I've nothing left, I'll look down at my hands and think that God will still grant me just enough strength to go out and earn enough to pay my taxes. And if I have to die of hunger, I'll die happy if only I know that I've paid my taxes. A man who doesn't pay his taxes is a good-for-nothing.'

Vojović sighed. 'They say that the government is oppressing the people.'

'That's the first I've heard of it. It can't be true. The Germans are our brothers; they wouldn't oppress us. They've set up German schools for us, to teach us to pray for them in German. And when you're sitting there nice and cosy in one of those schools, what kind of oppression is that? Who told you the government is oppressing the people, dimwit?'

Vojović cleared his throat in bewilderment. 'They take your sons away for the army,' he said, in the faint hope that he might yet get something out of Božetic.

'You're a proper fool,' said Mayor Božetic. 'How can they take my sons away for the army when all I've got is a daughter, who's married and lives in Mostar? And she hasn't any sons either, you blockhead!'

The next day, Officer Vojović went dejectedly back to Sarajevo and reported the results of his investigative expedition. 'He hasn't any brothers in Serbia; only Jovanović, the saddler in Šibak, has brothers in Serbia. One is a saddler in Kragujevac and the other is in Belgrade . . . And he goes on all the time about how glad he is to be living under an efficient administration.'

'Did he really say: "an efficient administration"?' asked the Chief Commissioner.

'Yes, Excellency,' replied Vojović, 'he said word for word: "I'm glad I can live under an efficient administration."'

'In that case,' said the Chief Commissioner, 'he's been making a fool of you.'

And Officer Vojović was discharged with ignominy from the Reports Department.   *1909–10*

Infantryman Trunec's Cap

At the beginning of October, a new recruit by the name of Trunec started his three years of military service in the infantry. He was a mountain of a man and his head rested proudly on a massive pair of shoulders. He had the neck of an ox and the head of a giant.

On the day he first arrived at the barracks, he went for a medical and was taken, with all the other recruits, before an NCO who questioned him, as he did everyone else, about his home circumstances. They do this in order to instil into our soldiers a feeling of trust towards the military. Then, having aroused their faith in the army, they took the recruits off to the Stores to get them kitted out.

The Quartermaster Sergeant scrutinised them one after the other and called out: 'Boots, No. 3, Trousers, 6, Tunic, No. 2.' Four corporals then brought boots, trousers and tunic to the recruit in question, whose sizes the QMS had estimated by eye, without bothering his head about whether the things would fit. So one man had boots in which he could have accommodated another two feet of his size, while another couldn't have got his feet into his boots to save his life, not even if he'd taken a plane and shaved half of each foot off. Another recruit could have got his elder brother into his trousers with him and yet another had a tunic into which he could have squeezed two more frames as skinny as his own. But this was the army and the number that the QMS called out was the one that applied. Then they were issued with their caps. These come in about six sizes, ranging from the biggest head to the smallest. The cap-issue was a shambles as well, but what can you do?

Then they all went to their barrack-room and got changed. It was a sight to reduce strong men to tears. A roomful of figures who had become unrecognisable one to the other. The hut was swarming with men whose hands had disappeared inside their tunics, men with their trousers dragging along the floor, men with their caps down over their ears. And on the other hand, there were men with their trousers up to their knees, so that you could see their underpants, arms protruding from the sleeves of tunics from the elbows down and in many cases, caps swaying precariously to and fro on their owners' heads. Where one part of the Company had a surplus, the other was deficient.

When the QMS caught sight of these interesting little groups, he nodded his head benevolently and said: 'There you are, lads, that's how variable the dimensions of the human body are. This man's got longer arms than he ought to have, that one has them shorter. It's the same with the legs. And the chest; well, it hardly bears thinking about. This one can't do his tunic up, and that one hangs inside his like a picture of the Crucifixion. But it'll all come out in the wash. You'll just have to exchange clothes amongst yourselves. And let me tell you, a soldier's got to look as if he's just come out of a bandbox; smartly turned out at all times. Anything funny about the way he looks, and he's on a charge.'

And so they exchanged boots, tunics, trousers and caps with their neighbours until there was just the one giant recruit, Trunec, left. He stuck out like a sore thumb in trousers that were too short for him and a tunic he couldn't do up; like a strange creature from an alien planet with a tiny cap cowering timorously on its head. The others, it's true, looked odd as well, but this one, Private Trunec, looked as if he had come from another world.

Trunec pleaded with them not to leave him in this state. The army has one answer to problems like this: 'Get on with it! Quick March!'

Trunec then turned to his corporal who was moved by his pleas and took him down to the Stores again where, after much searching, they did manage to find some bits and pieces of uniform that gave Trunec some sort of passing resemblance to a soldier. But the cap, alas! – the biggest cap they had – was swallowed up in that vast expanse of head like a grain of sand in the ocean.

And so it came to pass that the whole matter of his cap went all the way up to the Quartermaster-General's Office in Vienna.

It happened this way. The first duty of a soldier is to learn how to salute, by which means he shows respect to his superiors.

Private Trunec, with a cap that jumped about on his head like a ball bouncing about on the floor, could not with the best will in the world find the peak of his cap which, according to regulations, he had to touch when saluting.

These attempts of his to catch the peak of his cap were desperate affairs, for the slightest movement would send the cap slithering to the back of his head.

The sergeant was ready to tear his hair and the officer cursed and went puce with rage whenever, during these terrifying attempts at a salute, the wretched man's cap fell from his head to the ground.

In distraction, the red-faced Private Trunec would push it over one ear, which occasioned muffled laughter in the ranks and renewed outbursts of wrath on the part of the officer and the sergeant.

What were they to do with him?

Finally, the officer had the corporal take Private Trunec to the Company Office. Looking like a drunk, with his cap bobbing up and down, and ignorant of what was to befall, Trunec made his way with faltering steps to the Office.

When they got to the office, the duty clerk, on hearing the corporal's report, had Trunec taken to the Captain. The Captain took the report seriously. First of all, he asked Trunec whether he had water on the brain and when the latter said politely that No sir, he didn't have any water, Sir, the Captain ordered that the cap be soaked in water and forced on to Trunec's head. He said that this would cause the cap to stretch and that Trunec must keep it on his head for a whole day. To this end, Trunec was shut in the cells for twenty-four hours, so that no-one should disturb him (this, of course, was not a punishment).

Trunec sat there on his bunk, clinging devotedly to the cap on his head, until eventually he fell asleep with fatigue. When he got up next morning, the cap was lying beside him on the bunk, every bit as small and even more wrinkled. And this was the biggest cap the regiment had.

He put it back on his head and practised holding it in a balanced position, but it didn't do any good. The cap bounced about as it had on the previous day.

It had split and Trunec had to report to his Company Office a second time.

This time, the Captain took the matter even more seriously. He ordered the sergeant to take the measurements of the Trunec head. It turned out to have a circumference of sixty-two centimetres. Then the Captain said sternly to Trunec that the whole thing was going to have to go up to the Quartermaster-General's Office in Vienna. What did he mean by it, coming into the world with a head like that? Then he was dismissed. Outside, they rammed the cap back on his head and later it was re-sewn by the tailor and Trunec went on with his training, thankful not to have been put in the guardhouse.

II

After Trunec had gone, the Captain dictated a letter to the Company Clerk:

> To the Office of His Imperial Majesty's Quartermaster-General, Vienna:
>
> Sir,
>
>   The undersigned Third Company of the Twelfth Regiment respectfully requests the Quartermaster General's Office, in view of the fact that Infantryman Jan Trunec, born in Pelhřimov, domiciled in Kadan', possesses a head of abnormal size, to send a cap large enough to accommodate the dimensions of the head of the said infantryman.

Then the Captain signed the document with his own hand, a copy went into the files and the letter was received the next day by the Quartermaster-General's Office.

Two weeks later, Infantryman Trunec was called again to the Company Office, where he had his head measured yet once more, for that day a reply had arrived from the Quartermaster-General's Office in Vienna, to wit:

> To the Third Company, Twelfth Regiment:
>
>   With ref. doc. 6728/891 IIab/6721/345g III a 8 IV, the undersigned Quartermaster General's Office finds itself compelled to draw attention to the following:
>
>   The communication received from the Third Company of the Twelfth Regiment, No. 6728/891 IIab/6721/345g III a 8 IV in which a request is made to the Quartermaster-General's Office for the supply of a cap to Infantryman Jan Trunec of that same Company, domiciled in Kadan', born in Pelhřimov, because the aforesaid infantryman has a head of abnormal size, omits to give details of the dimensions of the head of the said infantryman. We request immediate notification of the aforesaid dimensions of the infantryman's abnormal head.
>
>   (....)
>
>   Commanding Officer,
>   Quartermaster-General's Office, Vienna

'Cor!' said the Company Clerk. 'You ain't 'alf giving us a 'ard time!' Then he wrote back that the head measured sixty-two centimetres and sent the letter off to Vienna. Two weeks later a new communication from Vienna arrived in the Company Office:

> The undersigned Quartermaster-General's Office in Vienna requests, with ref. document 6829/351/IIg IIId 3321 duly received here, information as to the date of birth of the said infantryman with the abnormal head and the year of service in which he currently stands, for the possibility that the head of the said infantryman might increase in size cannot be ruled out.

The Company Clerk notified them of the date of birth and that it was the first year of military service. Two months later, the following document arrived from Vienna:

> To the Third Company, Twelfth Regiment:
> We request herewith the immediate dispatch of the original cap issued to Infantryman Trunec, to prevent accounting difficulties and to enable us to send a cap in exchange.

Three months later, a new communication arrived:

> The undersigned Quartermaster-General's Office confirms herewith receipt of the original cap issued to Infantryman Trunec, which has arrived in a damaged condition. You are hereby ordered to conduct an enquiry for the purpose of establishing how the cap in question came to be damaged. On conclusion of the enquiry, the Quartermaster-General's Office will, in accordance with para. 16 of Army Supply Regulations, invite tenders for the provision of a new cap with a circumference of sixty-two cm. for the abnormal head of Infantryman Trunec.

III

Letter from the Third Company of the Twelfth Regiment to the Quartermaster-General's Office in Vienna:

> It has been established by an enquiry carried out by this Company that Infantryman Trunec received the cap which was sent to Vienna for

exchange in a completely undamaged condition. Since, however, as has been established by the testimony of witnesses, he did not treat it with the respect properly due to War Department property, he caused damage to it in consequence. The said infantryman has, however, died in the interim and we therefore request the return of the original cap issued to Jan Trunec, the infantryman with the abnormal head.

1909–10

Mr Kauble's Donation
In Aid of the Local Poor

Mr Kauble held the office of Father of the Poor in the Third Quarter. For the past twenty years he had devoted all his energies to the fulfilment of his duties. It was he, first and foremost, who decided the allocation of permits for the distribution of free coal to the poor; he was a member of the Municipal Board of Elders and of the Commission for Local Poor-Relief.

Fixed to each of the three doors of his flat was a metal plate bearing the legend: 'Contributor to Local Poor-Relief'.

These little signs did not cost him a penny, for he had a stock of them at home and handed them out to anyone who made an annual contribution of twenty crowns for the benefit of the local poor. Not that the beggars ever saw a brass farthing of it, for it was all gobbled up by the costs of poor-relief administration. The Poverty Officer drew a salary of 2,400 crowns a year and then there was an official who got 1,600 and an attendant who was paid a hundred crowns a month. The rest went on various outgoings, such as trips by members of the Poor-Relief Department to attend conferences on poor-relief. They hadn't enough left after that to do anything for the beggars.

At those houses where previously they had been given alms, their attention was now drawn to the little sign on the door which said: 'Contributor to Local Poor-Relief'.

It was a good idea, then, to call a conference on Ways of Reducing Street-Begging. A local journal had previously conducted a survey of methods by which the level of begging could be brought down.

A number of letters came in, pointing out how widespread begging was in other towns.

So shrewd were these comments, so self-evidently true, that there was nothing for it but to call a conference on the Reduction of Street-Begging.

During the week before the conference, Mr Kauble, the Father of the Poor, roamed the streets of the Quarter, stopping beggars and urging them to stop begging. He also drew the attention of the Police to a number of beggars. It was a week of fruitful reflection on ways in which he might come forward at the conference with some scheme to reduce the extent of begging or eliminate it altogether.

The conference was also attended by a police-representative and from the District Sheriff's Office came the District Sheriff himself, who fell asleep during the Mayor's address. And during this address, the police-representative assiduously cleaned and filed his nails and Chaplain Bláha, representing the local Church, perused for the fifth time the constitution of a certain Firemen's Association that had happened to fall into his hands.

The Mayor's address made an embarrassing impression.

He kept on saying: 'And now, we shall strive to defeat begging. Now, our aim will be to force it into retreat; now is the time to go on the offensive against it. I take as my point of departure today the principle that we ought to take severe measures against it.' He went on like that for a full half-hour and ended by saying: 'If any gentleman present has any kind of concrete proposal to make, let him please now put it forward.'

Up got the Father of the Poor in the Third Quarter, Mr Kauble.

His face at that moment, as he gazed out at the solemn faces of the members of the conference, was aglow with enthusiasm.

He had prepared himself to tell them everything that he had been turning over in his mind during the last week and thinking over in his bed at night. It's pleasant, as you lie in your comfortable feather-bed, to contemplate the poverty of your neighbours.

Before the conference began, he had got himself a litre of wine and that warm glow in his stomach was now spreading to his heart and soul and he began to speak emotionally about the fate of the widows and orphans.

The District Sheriff slept on and the police-representative yawned.

'Widows and orphans,' cried Mr Kauble in a tone of desperation, 'must be protected. Protect the widows and orphans from ruin. Gentlemen,' his voice rose to a crescendo that made the Town Hall's conference-chamber shake, 'something must be done to help them, something immediate to rescue them from destitution. Gentlemen, I am firmly resolved to make a donation.'

Upon this, the District Sheriff woke up. Sixty pairs of eyes gazed in eagerness and amazement into the eyes of Mr Kauble.

'The best man among us,' whispered the Mayor to his neighbours.

'Yes, a donation,' cried the Father of the Poor in a voice throbbing with exaltation. 'A donation which will ease the lot of at least one poor widow. I hereby announce the donation of a barrel-organ.' A silence fell all around.

'The best man among us has lost his marbles,' whispered the Mayor to those around him, while Mr Kauble, his eyes flashing, drew a sheet of paper from his pocket and continued:

'I, Antonín Kauble, Father of the Poor in the Third Quarter, house- and estate-owner, President of the Antonín Kauble Charitable Foundation, etc, do hereby make bold to communicate to the public the competitive grant of one barrel-organ to the poor of this town. Application for this grant may be made to the Parish Officer by any blind widow of sixty years and upwards who can furnish evidence of utter integrity, piety, total incapacity for hard labour, and honesty. Evidence of age, death-certificate and certificate of domicile of the spouse and the testimony of an eye-witness should be sent, together with the application, to the Poor-Relief section of the local Municipal Office or to the donor, Antonín Kauble, Father of the Poor. The barrel-organ is to be conferred for life and the beneficiary will have the obligation to pray once a week for the donor's family at early mass.'

When the Father of the Poor had finished speaking, silence fell once more, to be broken eventually by the Mayor, who asked: 'May I venture a comment, Mr Kauble?'

He rose:

'In the name of the whole Poor-Relief Commission, I would like to thank Mr Kauble for his selfless initiative in the interest of alleviating the misery of the poor. I give thanks to you in the name of the whole town, in the name of my suffering fellow-citizens. Our thanks, our ardent thanks to you!'

He ended on an emotional note and the District Sheriff, stepping over to Mr Kauble, offered his hand in a demonstrative manner and said: 'I too, most worthy Sir, must thank you. This example has shown me that the self-denial of the leaders of society in this town knows no bounds. Be assured that I shall not forget your noble action for the benefit of the local poor.'

The days that followed were for Mr Kauble days of pure happiness.

The news of his benefaction was reported in the newspapers and a few days later, in a display-case in a musical instrument-dealer's shop in the main street, there appeared a barrel-organ with the clearly printed inscription: 'Donated by Mr Antonín Kauble, Father of the Poor'.

Then Mr Kauble had his photograph taken, standing beside the barrel-organ and resting one hand on it.

He had a postcard made from this photograph and became more popular than ever. His happiness was complete and his self-esteem touched new heights. The District Sheriff was giving him the nicest smiles. There could be no doubt that some distinction would be conferred on him at the earliest opportunity.

All this happened shortly before a Distinguished Person honoured the town with a visit.

In the full consciousness of his own worthiness, Mr Kauble went along to the General Audience.

'I will present the postcard with myself standing beside the barrel-organ to the Distinguished Visitor.' This was his final thought as he entered the audience-chamber.

Then all the lights went out for him.

The Distinguished Visitor stood facing him, smiling.

'Anton Kauble, Most Gracious Highness,' he stammered, like a good Czech, in German and added, as he presented the postcard: 'Anton Kauble and his barrel-organ, Father of the Poor.'

'Yes, I am always a Father to the poor and needy,' said the Distinguished Visitor benevolently, went across to his equerry and said something to him, whereupon the equerry came up to Mr Kauble, gave him a gold twenty-crown piece and said in an official tone: 'The audience is at an end.'

To which the Distinguished Visitor added in a friendly voice: 'Don't give up hope, old chap! An old soldier can always get by, even with a barrel-organ.'

The Father of the Poor tottered out through the door, and an hour later the news had gone round the whole of the Third Quarter that Mr Kauble had taken a stick and smashed his donation in aid of the poor to smithereens.

1909–10

The Immoral Calendars

I

From nine o'clock at night till one in the morning, time had hung heavy on the hands of Aleš, the duty officer at the police-station. How, he thought, was he going to hold out till six o'clock (when he would be relieved), sitting over the paperwork and the newspapers when, by a dirty trick of Fate, the men on duty couldn't play his favourite card-game?

So he lay on his bed, lit his pipe and talked politics. At moments like this he would take a strong line. He became an Austrian Cato, stern and unwavering and full of distrust for the Italians, which he vented in the most forceful terms. The men lying on their beds beside him, who lacked a definitive position, listened respectfully.

'Under no circumstances should anyone imagine that the Triple Alliance will hold. Trent and Trieste will become bones of contention one day.' He sighed and looked around for a match. When somebody had given him one, he lit up again and announced that in Milan and Turin, and indeed in Rome as well, they were burning the Austrian flag at every opportunity. But they'd get their come-uppance one day. They were ripe for another Custozza, those ruffians. His agitation increased and the young policeman Pavelka, who had dropped off, began to whistle through his nose. He was woken up by the Chief, who was shouting that there were bound to be complications. All Austrian citizens . . .

In through the door came Constable Dekl, back from the beat to report: '*Melde gehorsam, nix Neues. Ich habe ein* naughty calendar *konfisziert.*' The official expression disappeared from Dekl's face at that point and he announced triumphantly: 'A king-size *Schweinerei, Herr Wachkommandant.* Some really juicy stuff. Filthy pictures to bring joy to your heart!'

He put the bundle down on a chair. And at that moment, the Chief's boredom vanished. 'Let's have it out, then, this muck of yours!'

The constable undid the bundle and gave the Chief a copy of the confiscated item, while all the policemen clustered round.

'*Herrgott!*' said one spontaneously, looking at the title-page. 'There's a pair of thighs for you!'

'There you are!' said the Chief. 'That's the sort of thing our young people are supposed to look at! Young people not yet out of school!' His voice softened. 'Blimey! Look at this other one in the picture here! Devil take her eyes! She's stark naked!'

'And blow me!' said Constable Dekl, 'there's some nice things further on.'

'This one's not bad either!'

'Bollocks, man! The one next to her is prettier, and spicier!'

'This little beauty's got fuller hips. And the way she's posing on the couch is a bit of all right. Filthy swine! How dare they draw things like this?'

'*Herr Wachkommandant*, just read the poem underneath. That's not bad either.'

'It's pretty good; but there's a *double entendre* here. They ought to be ashamed to write stuff like that and print it! There are schoolchildren drinking in this bloody . . . what d'you call it?'

'Pornography, *Herr Wachkommandant*,' said Pavelka, supplying the missing word.

'Shocking!' said Constable Mika. 'But good stuff. These trousers are well drawn.'

'And the joke's not bad: Do you like me better with trousers, darling, or without?'

'Without, I would say, wouldn't you?' said the Chief, turning to the other policemen with a twinkle in his eye. 'The things these filthy pigs think up!'

'Go on, *Herr Wachkommandant*, just have a look at the last page but one. The dancer in the baths. Not only is she completely naked, but the attendant is handing her a sheet.'

'That's nice. They ought to stamp on things like this most severely. I say, I reckon that if you go round all the newsagents, you'll find more of the same. Commissioner Peroutka is going to have a good time tomorrow!'

II

'Beg leave to report, Commissar, that following instructions, we went round the newsagents yesterday and confiscated some calendars with really filthy material in them. I've brought one along. I would particularly draw your attention to the last picture but one, the dancer in the baths. And then that woman on the couch. The title-picture as well. Not only is it an offence against morality, but I think the Chief Commissar would like it. I'll take the liberty of sending a copy upstairs as well. If you would be so very kind as to take a close look at the shameless bit I've marked with blue pencil. That's a serious matter. Wherever I've marked a page, you'll find first-class examples of lewd material. If you'd care to look on page thirty, you'll find a dirty poem. A special delicacy is "Intimacies of the Harem". Not only are there crass offences against morality in the text; the illustrations are a real treat. Saucy little Mohammedan girls being looked after by some poor devil of a eunuch.'

'Wow!' said Commissar Peroutka, when he had perused the contents. 'You must show this to our Councillor as well. He enjoys looking at things like this.'

III

The calendars went down well. The Chief Commissar of Police took two and the Councillor three. The copy-clerks had one each. The rest were distributed about the police-station. The police investigation into this immoral material was a very thorough one. And precisely by ensuring that reading-matter like this did not fall into the hands of those for whom it was unsuitable, they acted as guardians of public morals.

1910

A Psychiatric Puzzle

I

It was about two o'clock in the morning and Mr Hurych was on his way home from a meeting of the Total Abstainers Society which had been held in a restaurant in the Malá Strana. The reason why that meeting had gone on so long was that it had been discussing the resignation of the society's president, who had become involved in an ugly affair. He stood convicted, in fact, of having drunk a glass of *pilsner* in a certain restaurant. As a man of honour, he had stepped down.

Mr Hurych, then, was going home across the Charles Bridge. He walked along full of the heart-warming assurance that he was working for the good of humanity. In his stomach, true, he still felt the coolness of soda-water, but a little higher, there beat a warm, an ardently philanthropic heart - a heart that would have been within an ace of succumbing to fatty degeneration if his doctor had not told him to cut out the beer. And now, he was an abstainer of some six months' standing; he had thrown himself wholeheartedly into the fight against alcohol, become an active member of an abstainers' association, a subscriber to Humanitarian Causes, a student of Esperanto and a vegetarian.

His musings were interrupted by a shout from the river. This was exactly the kind of nocturnal cry that young poets love and that brings them in sixteen hellers a time, for that is the going rate for a line of verse in which a cry comes floating up from the river in the stillness of the night, mysteriously, out of the unknown.

Mr Hurych leaned over the balustrade of the bridge and called down to the surface of the Vltava, full of a premonition of disaster: 'Was there something you wanted?'

At that moment, as he stood leaning his philanthropic heart over the side of the bridge, he could think of nothing cleverer to say.

And at just the time when Mr Hurych was peering keenly down into the water, a hairdresser called Bílek was proceeding across the bridge in the direction of the Malá Strana.

This gentleman, though he was no abstainer and certainly not on that particular day, still had a heart no less noble, no less imbued with love for his fellow-man than that of Mr Hurych. A heart of gold, a selfless heart.

One swift glance told him that Mr Hurych was leaning over the side of the bridge in a suspicious manner. Mr Bílek was a man of action. Softly as a cat, swiftly as a lynx, he approached Mr Hurych from behind, seized him by the arm and attempted to wrestle him to the ground. Mr Hurych, though, was not coming quietly: he grabbed the unknown man by the neck and to shouts of 'Police!' these two high-minded men grappled with each other, while the hairdresser cried out: 'Calm yourself! What was it that drove you to despair?'

The police-patrol came trotting up and Mr Bílek, clasping Mr Hurych in his arms with all his strength, panted out as they approached: 'Officers, this gentleman was about to jump into the river and I've saved him.'

Four highly experienced hands now took charge of Mr Hurych and grasped him under the armpits and in a fatherly voice, one policeman started to try to talk Mr Hurych out of his suicidal frame of mind.

Mr Hurych was taken aback by this state of affairs and shouted, like a man in a paroxysm of hysteria: 'It's all a mistake, gentlemen!'

Then he burst into a strained and unnatural laughter and repeated: 'You're mistaken, gentlemen; I really wasn't going to jump into the river.'

He was interrupted by the high-minded barber, who was walking behind them: 'This isn't the first time I've saved people when they were trying to jump into the river, but no-one so far has struggled as violently as you did. It's plain to see, you're terribly upset. Why, you've torn my waistcoat.'

Then the other policeman started droning into Mr Hurych's ear: 'Good Heavens! Where would we be if everybody had to take his own life as soon as some little thing went wrong? It'll all come right again. Whatever it was that made you so upset, it'll sort itself out. And in the morning, when you've cooled down, you'll see that it's a beautiful world in spite of everything.'

'It's a beautiful world,' said the policeman on Mr Hurych's right. 'If everyone were to want to jump into the water every time he got some bee in his bonnet, half the world would have to drown itself.'

Meanwhile, Mr Bílek was tugging at Mr Hurych's coat and adding, with much emphasis: 'Just so that you know who it was that saved your life, remember, when you come to yourself, that the name is Bílek and that I'm a hairdresser in Smíchov.'

Once again Mr Hurych began to cry out hysterically: 'I beg you, gentlemen, let me go; really, I didn't have anything in mind: I was just leaning over the balustrade because it seemed to me that someone was calling out down on the river.'

'I beg your pardon!' retorted the barber. 'So you weren't going to jump, eh? I've had some experience of cases like this, my friend! I only have to look at someone and I know straight away whether he's going to jump or not. If you hadn't intended to jump, old son, you wouldn't have put up such a fierce struggle. When you remember all this in the morning, you'll thank God that your Guardian Angel sent me your way.'

Mr Hurych's patience finally gave way and he turned and hurled a number of coarse insults into the face of that noble and selfless man. More in sorrow than in anger, Mr Bílek addressed the policemen: 'That's the reward a man gets for doing a kindness! When this gentleman comes to himself in the morning he'll be ashamed of the way he repaid his rescuer.'

Mr Hurych made an attempt to throw himself at the hairdresser, but desisted when the policemen told him they would send for the drunk-cart.

As they neared the police-station, he made one last attempt to clear the whole thing up: 'Why won't you believe me? I swear to you that it's all an accident.'

'Now, now, calm down,' said the policemen soothingly, 'when you've had a good night's sleep and cleared all this out of your head, you'll see the world with completely different eyes.'

'Oh, my God!' wailed Mr Hurych.

II

There is a whole clutch of mental illnesses which are accompanied by suicide-attempts, such as *paralysa progressiva*, paranoia, melancholia, various types of mania, hysteria and psychosis.

Police-doctors who are called to treat would-be suicides use, as the most reliable psychiatric aid, the question-and-answer system.

The answers that an attempted suicide gives serve as a guide to the doctor in diagnosing the specific type of mental illness, which will always be accompanied by confusion of concepts and ideas.

In this case too a police-doctor was sent for to examine Mr Hurych's mental condition.

Before he arrived, the Station Officer interviewed the altruistic barber and wrote a report.

He too could not resist the temptation to lighten Mr Hurych's gloom by pointing to the delights that the world has to offer.

'It'll all come right again, Sir; everything will turn out all right, even if it's an unhappy love-affair. It'll pass. It's true what they say: "There's more than one fish in the sea." When you've cooled down, in the morning, you'll want to go and thank Mr Bílek most warmly for having saved your life. And if it's some kind of domestic upset, why not move out? Don't take it so much to heart. And if you're in financial difficulties of some kind (for I can't see into your circumstances), well, an honest man can get by. Work gives a man dignity!'

And what reply did Mr Hurych make to all this? He covered his face with his hands and cried out: 'For the sweet love of Christ, I tell you I wasn't going to do anything!'

And then Mr Bílek was on at him again: 'I am Bílek, the hairdresser from Smíchov. You can tell me what drove you to it.'

Mr Hurych began to cry.

III

The police-doctor arrived and said: 'Bring in the examinee.'

Mr Hurych was brought in. His face was white with fear, his lips pale, his hair dishevelled.

'Why were you going to jump into the river?'

'I swear that I wasn't.'

'Don't deny it. We have Mr Bílek and the policemen as witnesses. When they saved your life, you struggled violently.'

'This is terrible,' lamented Mr Hurych.

'Tell me, why does the sun set?'

'Please, doctor, I beg you!'

'Can you tell me the names of some independent states in Asia?'

'Doctor, please!'

'What is six times twelve?'

But at that point, Mr Hurych's self-control deserted him and instead of saying 'seventy-two', he thumped the police-doctor round the ear as hard as he could.

In the morning, they took him off to the lunatic asylum, where he has been detained for the last eighteen months, because the doctors have not yet been able to detect in him that awareness that he is mentally ill which, according to the psychiatric text-books, is the first sign of an improvement in a patient's mental condition.

1911

A Sporting Sketch

Oh, what gladness fills your pounding heart as you read the words: 'Our small nation has lived, in the three days just past, through moments of joyful anticipation, high excitement and very special pride.'

And your excitement mounts as you go on to read in the following lines that the Genius of Slavdom has put an end to the suffering of the people and you read of the days of Hus and of Comenius and of the spreading of the nation's cultural wings.

And what it's all about is the glorious appearance among us of a troupe of Scottish entertainers.

'It was from history that we drew the support, the strength of will and the pride that after two centuries awakened our good people to a new and beautiful life.'

And it is for this very reason that a handful of itinerant professionals are being fêted in the City Hall.

'The truth, for which the best of our sons sacrificed their blood and their possessions, has brought forth the most exquisite of blossoms.' After Dobrovský, Šafařík, Jungmann* and a whole string of names from the National Revival, along come Slavie and put three goals past the paid artists of Aberdeen who, against the descendants of the people which groaned for centuries under the iron heel of the usurper, could manage no more than two.

The trail of Germanisation stretches across the purely Czech regions and if you find yourself on the other side of Turnov, the man in the ticket-office won't give you a ticket for love or money if you ask for it in Czech. In the Czech enclaves, outrageous things are being done to the Czech school system . . . but then, along come Aberdeen and Slavie beat them 3–2.

What balm for our cultural wounds! The Town Council wheels out its conveyances for these paid gladiators, ferries them around in carriages and entertains them; a banquet is arranged and Anglo-Czech relations are firmly cemented.

* See Introduction, note 2 on these figures and, later in the story, Havlíček.

If a sword-swallower from the island of Cuba comes here, all the talk will be of Czech–Cuban relations. Once again, they'll take the sword-swallower to the City Hall, and there he'll be given an album of views of Prague, a banquet will be arranged in his honour, he'll ride up to Hradčany in a carriage with the Deputy Mayor and be made to feel at home everywhere. No-one will ask him who he is exactly; it'll be enough for us that he's from Cuba and good at swallowing swords.

And this will assuredly be the occasion for our papers to write about the Cubans' struggle for independence and to say that there are few fields in which we too could not excel. So now we are showing the Aberdonian entertainers the monuments in the City Hall.

And the next day, our papers will report the dubious intelligence that there are some good minds among the Aberdonians as well, for there are three former university students among their number.

We have given an official reception at the City Hall for eleven mercenaries from Aberdeen who don't give a damn whether they're dribbling a ball in Prague or Budapest, or in Vienna or Brussels maybe and who, just like all the other employees, take their wages, their pay from the management of Aberdeen Ltd (Directors, William Jaffrey, James Philip and the dentist Joseph Ellis Milne). These gentlemen draw a hundred thousand crowns a year in salary and pay their employees good wages. Just like any Count who keeps a staff of jockeys to win prizes for him. And so here we are in the City Hall in our best black coats, holding an official reception for the paid employees of Aberdeen Ltd.

And we lavish flattering phrases on them. The Deputy Mayor speaks of the proud sons of the Scottish mountains, who haven't a clue what he's on about: how could they, when all they know how to do is head a ball, kick the cover off it, pass the bouncing ball from one to the other and hurl themselves at the opposition? Why, when that is all they know, do they show them pictures in the City Hall, talk about the Council of Constance, the execution of the Czech gentry or the awakening of the Czech people?

Then they hear the name 'Havlíček', and since Havlíček is constantly being mentioned they have to ask: How many did he get?

And the questions come in a rush: When did Havlíček last play for Slavie? Did he have a good shot?

And then they hear someone going on about Hus, upon whom the mantle of their own Wyclif has fallen, after which those selfsame people who talk so enthusiastically about Hus take them out in boats to see the

Saint John Fireworks.

'This is in memory of Saint John Nepomucene.'

'How many did he get?'

And then they take them out to a party and sing them 'The Maidens of the Castle', the Czech anthem.

To which they reply with a Scots song about a pretty sutler-lass, the contents of which are no whit less salty than our soldiers' song *When we went to Jaroměř*. Nobody understands what it's about and there is great enthusiasm all round.

The eleven professional entertainers from Aberdeen leave for home.

They've won some and lost some. They've headed, they've dribbled, they've scored and they've passed. Besides their pay, they're carrying with them in their cases some medals which they had presented to them in the City Hall.

Their heads are in a whirl from all the things they've seen and what bothers them most is that they never found out how many that Charlie Havlíček scored and what team he played for.

While we, in our papers, give those eleven professional entertainers the following rousing send-off: 'Gone are the days of meek submission; we long to stand strong beside the strong and to make it impossible that we should ever again suffer the terrible shame of bondage. Let us take an example from these proud sons of the Scottish mountains who dedicate all their strength to the service of the homeland they love so dearly.'

Oh yes, for a wage of two pounds sterling a day, which is the equivalent of forty-eight crowns . . .

Mary Queen of Scots, now: how many did she get?

1911

My Career as Editor of an Animal Magazine

The sea-serpent season lasts only a few weeks in the daily papers, but as editor of the magazine *Animal World*, I had it all year round. Over the years, successive editors of *Animal World* had churned out all sorts of stuff about animals and when I took up the editorship in my turn, I found that there wasn't an animal in the world that hadn't already been written about in *Animal World*.

So I was forced to invent animals and this was much less like hard work than writing about animals that had been discovered ages ago.

My first exploit was the discovery of the Gruesome Guzzler, called 'Ajajoro' by the inhabitants of the Fortunate Isles, an animal that lives in the sea from ten o'clock in the morning till four o'clock in the afternoon. The rest of the day it spends on the Fortunate Isles gobbling up children. This is what I wrote:

> This animal is not enormous, but its gruesomeness makes it extremely formidable. Dr Everich the scientist, well-known to our readers as a friend of this journal, has sent us this description of the Gruesome Guzzler from San Francisco:
>
> 'Judging by its bone-structure, it belongs to the lizard family. I suspect that it is the only species that has been preserved down to our own day from the age of the great lizards like Ichthyosaurus and other gigantic antediluvian animals. On the underbelly, beneath its armour-plating, it has feather-cases that it rubs together when agitated, producing a racket that can be heard two English miles away.
>
> 'I managed to snap up a specimen of this monster at the expense of a native boy. Having been placed in a large bamboo cage, it ate up the whole of the cage and half of the hut that contained the cage during the night and escaped into the interior, where it was finally shot with a machine-gun. In its stomach, they found a Major of the Civil Guard. The wretched man had starved to death imprisoned within the bony walls of the creature's stomach, on which he had written in pencil: "Please convey my last greetings to my poor wife."
>
> 'Interestingly enough, the flesh of this monster is very popular with the natives. I first tasted this meat on the island of Kalalo. Its taste

resembles that of pork. When cooked, the meat has a pinkish colour. The eyes are large. The brain-cavity is full of brain. How the creature reproduces, I have not yet been able to ascertain. I am sending a photograph by the same post.'

Thus far the account of our friend. We print the photograph on a separate page. [I had someone work up a reproduction of an Ichthyosaurus.]

This was an auspicious start to my editorial career. Two school-teachers immediately took out two-year subscriptions and I buckled down with a will to the job of animal-production.

Since turning out completely new animals all the time is very difficult, I went into the world of whales in the next number. I discovered the Sulphur-bellied Whale, which roams the seas around New Greenland and then, just to add a bit of spice, I began to regale the public with fascinating titbits from the life of the animal kingdom.

The hippopotamus, I wrote, likes it when the natives blow up its nostrils; ants are susceptible to the charms of *La Traviata*. And at the same time, I published a long article explaining how you can prevent buzzing around buffaloes by smearing the gadflies with turpentine.

Another peculiar fact of animal life is that snails recognise the points of the compass and crawl eastwards when the wind blows from the west. Termites build their nests in such a way that the sharp edge is turned towards the Trade Winds, so that they cut through the wind, and this constitutes a great boon for the whole of northern Australia.

One science-teacher was so taken with these odd facts that he became a subscriber to *Animal World* and wrote, in an enthusiastic letter announcing this scientific decision, that he would spread news of our journal far and wide for it had opened up new animal worlds for him.

Fired by this success, I composed for the next number an extremely eye-catching article entitled: 'A Practical Guide to the Keeping of Werewolves'. For the first month, I wrote, werewolves have to be fed on ox-blood and this should continue until the sixth month, when the ox-blood should be replaced with draff. Werewolves reproduce every other year, in the month of July. During the period when they are mating (or wolving), you have to keep out of their way, unless you are prepared to be sprayed with a liquid one part in twenty-five of pure spirits and that smells of musk. Werewolves are very affectionate, good and faithful companions and they make vigilant watch-wolves, so that they are in every respect capable of replacing dogs, over which they have the advantage of exceptional intelligence and of self-control.

Two breeds of werewolf are distinguished: the Siberian and the Manchurian. The former breed has silvery fur, the fur of the latter is tinged with gold.

The article was a great success. A week, perhaps, after its appearance, a lady dressed in black turned up at the office, asking if we could supply her with a pair of young Siberian werewolves.

I was not in the office at the time and when the clerk (who hadn't the faintest idea what a werewolf is) took her there, she spoke to the assistant. We sold all kinds of animals on the side and the assistant, who knew as little about werewolves as did the clerk, said: 'Of course, Madam, we can get you a fine pair. We don't have any in stock here, because we keep only dogs in this location, but we've got some in our nursery out in the country. They're about four months old.'

She said she wanted six-month-old werewolves.

'Of course, Madam,' said the helpful assistant. 'We've got six-month-old werewolves as well, nicer than the four-month-old ones.'

'Are they Siberian?'

'We only do the Siberian.'

'Do they bite?'

'Oh dear no, Madam, our werewolves are completely tame. They're like children and they run round after their masters like little dogs. It's really extraordinary.'

'Very well,' said the lady in mourning. 'I found the article in your magazine very interesting, for I'm very fond of animals. When I was talking about it with my father, my little five-year-old, Karlíček, decided he wouldn't have anything else but a werewolf. Every day, when he wakes up in the morning, he cries: "Mummy, I want a werewolf!" I've even come all the way to Prague from Olomouc.'

'As soon as the weather's fine enough, Madam, we'll send you the werewolves on approval,' said the helpful assistant. 'If you would kindly let me have your address.'

A fortnight went by and then a man with long white moustaches appeared in the office.

'I've come about the werewolves,' he said sternly. 'My daughter ordered them and they haven't been sent yet. All our friends are looking forward to their arrival very much. I would like to see them straight away.'

'It's not possible to send them at the moment,' I said in my most ingratiating manner. 'The Austrian authorities have banned the importation of werewolves because the Trade Agreement between Austria and Russia hasn't been renewed yet. As soon as the Agreement has been renewed, we'll let you know.'

Some time later, I was out for a stroll in a park in Olomouc. A lady in black sat down on the seat beside me. She had a fine young boy on her lap and he was crying furiously. This made me nervous and as I walked away, I heard the little lad say tearfully to his mother: 'Mummy, I want my werewolf; Mummy, when will the werewolf come?'

I hurried away. In my pocket, I had a letter from a certain farmer in Bohemia who wrote that (in accordance with the advice given in *Animal World*) he had smeared the gadflies with turpentine (when he could get at them), but that his cows were still buzzing, and so he was coming to the office to pay me a visit.

I had a number of such letters in my pocket, among them one from a teacher who wrote that he had spent fourteen days in the observation of snails to find out whether they recognise the points of the compass and that now he was going to pay me a friendly visit to inform himself of the breed of snail involved.

Since I was in Olomouc when I came face to face with the little boy who wanted a werewolf, you will have come to the conclusion that I had fled from these experts in natural history to Moravia, where I plan to start a new nature-magazine in which I shall write about the intellectual capacities of the centipede.

1911

The Official Zeal of Mr Štěpán Brych, Toll-Collector on a Bridge in Prague

It can be asserted with absolute confidence that anyone who set foot on one of the bridges of Prague with the intention of proceeding across it was conscious of the solemnity of that moment. The sternly official faces of the men sitting inside and standing outside the toll-booth, the grave and dignified figure of the policeman standing in the thoroughfare and the placard outside the booth with its cold recital of the complete range of charges that applied equally to every man and beast that ventured onto those bridges, all this inspired a feeling of sublime awe. And looking more closely at those figures outside the booth, men impervious to corruption even by the seductive smile of womanhood, you felt the urge to kiss the hand that stretched out towards you, ready to receive your kreuzer. You sensed the love they bore towards the City Council, their sense of official duty, their incorruptibility and when you recalled that according to the law, these men in their flat official caps were protected by the sections covering the pursuit and punishment of all those guilty of the Molestation of an Official Person, then you delayed no longer but hat in hand, deposited your kreuzer into the palms of those Implacable Ones, the Brutuses of the City of Prague.

Pre-eminent among these was Štěpán Brych, the toll-collector on the Emperor-Franz-Joseph Bridge.

Every 'civilian' (non-official person) who wished to cross the bridge was subjected to the hawk-like scrutiny of those official eyes.

He would brook no banter, tolerate no delay.

As soon as some civilian (official persons do not pay bridge-tolls), some idiot of a civilian found himself a nose-length away from the outstretched hand of Štěpán Brych, there was no quarter given, no excuse taken. You paid up or you were lost beyond redemption.

A wave of Štěpán Brych's hand, and the policeman at the entrance to the bridge knew all he needed to know.

He would approach, his hand on his revolver. Štěpán Brych would indicate the person who was not forthcoming with his dues and utter the simple phrase: 'Take him in!'

And the policeman would grasp this person by the shoulder and say with equal simplicity: 'You coming quietly, or do I have to persuade you?'

Most people chose the first method of getting to the police-station.

There, the arrestee would be stripped, searched, measured, photographed, interrogated and placed in solitary confinement and in a day or at most a week it would have been ascertained whether he did in fact live at the address that he had given. Then they would either let him go or, if he had given any sign of dissatisfaction with all these legal procedures, send him to the Provincial High Court on Charles Square whence, once he had served his term, he would be compulsorily returned to his parish of origin. All of which was a comparatively light penalty to pay for a crime that the prisoner had attempted to perpetrate against the financial interest of the Buildings Department of Prague City Council. And the Marat of the Prague bridges, toll-collector Štěpán Brych, sat calmly watching as all this went on.

One day, Councillor Pojsl, the Head of the Buildings Department, came up to the toll-booth and said to Mr Štěpán Brych: 'Would you let me across the bridge without paying, old chap? I'm in a hurry to get to Smíchov and I've left my purse at home.'

Mr Štěpán Brych recognised his Chief, of course he did. He had a great liking and respect for him. And now, a fierce struggle broke out between affection for his Chief and devotion to his official duty.

The City Councillor stepped across the borderline denoted by the abruptly extended hand and Štěpán Brych tugged at Mr Pojsl's coat. Duty had prevailed.

'Back you come, or you pay a kreuzer,' he said in a dry official tone.

'Not on your life!' Štěpán Brych signed to the policeman who was lying in wait beside the toll-booth like a spider waiting for a fly, and called out that simple phrase of his: 'Take him in!'

And when the policeman, after his customary conjuration: 'You coming quietly or do I have to persuade you?' was leading the City Councillor away, a tear appeared in Brutus's eye and for the first time in his life, Štěpán Brych wept.

A fortnight later, a moving little ceremony was held in the Central Office of the Buildings Section. The Council had awarded a bronze medal for faithful service to Mr Štěpán Brych, collector of bridge-tolls, for having challenged City Councillor Pojsl himself (who had not been compulsorily returned to his office of origin in the City Council after his little problem).

This distinction made Štěpán Brych stricter than ever.

On the night of 2nd May of the same year, he was standing by the National Theatre on the right bank of the river when all of a sudden, what seemed like the figure of a man ran at full pelt past the toll-booth and across the bridge. There was no policeman on the bridge, as the officer was just taking some non-payer to the police-station, upon which Štěpán Brych set off after the offender, shouting: 'Stop! I want a kreuzer from you! There's a toll to pay here!' The unknown man seemed not to hear and raced on. After him dashed Štěpán Brych, calling into the darkness: 'Police! Grab him, he's got to pay a kreuzer!' Then they were in the Malá Strana, careering down the Ujezd, across Radetzky Square, down Valdštýn Street, on and on round the Chotek Gardens. The terrified stranger in the lead and Mr Štěpán Brych struggling along in his wake, shouting in a loud voice: 'You there! Give me that kreuzer, or I'll shoot!'

And on they went, up past the Dejvice Gate, along the Podbaba Road and when the moon came out, the fleeing man looked round for his pursuer and saw a man in the cap of an officer of the City Council, foaming at the mouth and rolling his eyes in a manner horrible to behold. Seized by a mortal fear, he ran to the river and, to save himself, leaped into the stream.

A second splash, and Štěpán Brych was swimming after the escaping criminal.

In the middle of the river, he caught up with him and with a cry of: 'Give me that kreuzer!' took him in a firm grip.

A huge wave swept them both into a whirlpool.

Three days later, two drowned men, locked in a convulsive embrace, were dragged out of the Vltava at Klecany.

In the clenched fist of one of the corpses, they found a kreuzer. And this was the body of Štěpán Brych who had succeeded, in his death-throes, in extracting a kreuzer from the pocket of the man he had pursued.

From that time, the Vltava has been haunted between Podbaba and Podhoří.

Every midnight, a voice can be heard crying out of the water: 'Give me a kreuzer!'

The ghost of Štěpán Brych walks the bed of the River Vltava.

1911

The Sad Fate of the Station Mission

The Countess Julia was a very virtuous young lady, a fact that means a great deal in the depraved state of today's morals. At the age of eighteen, with a heart still untarnished, she could talk as proficiently about prostitution and the ways in which it could be rooted out as if she herself had experienced all the hardships endured by fallen women in the Houses of Ill Fame. Her mother, the Princess Boldierová, had gathered round her a group of ladies who represented the flower of moral purity from both the aristocratic and the middle classes and they indulged in frequent deliberations, in the presence of the innocent Julia, on ways of protecting young girls and preventing them from being lured into Houses of Shame. Their first concern was for inexperienced girls who hadn't an inkling of the snares that lie in wait for them in the big city, any more than they had of the traps being laid for them by the company gathered around Princess Boldierová.

For Mrs Waldsteinová, the Commercial Councillor's wife, had proposed that girls from the country should be warned at the railway station itself of the dangers that threatened them, as they set foot in the city. And with this proposal, she got old Baroness Richterová into trouble. The latter made her way to the railway station one day, to meet the train from Tábor, and accosted a strapping young country wench who had just arrived with the words: 'Where are you going? Do you have a position? Do you have any money? Do you have any relatives in Prague?' The girl eyed her for a while as if she were a lunatic and then told the Baroness very firmly to leave her alone. 'Leave me alone, you old witch, or I'll thump you!' The worthy Baroness heard no more, for she fell down in a faint and has talked with a stutter ever since.

Later, at Princess Boldierová's, when she had stammered out the tale of how she had got on, Mrs Zapp, who had made her mark with a book for young girls on the sinful nature and harmful effects of dancing, proposed that they should organise a Railway Station Protection Service and that ladies who were willing to undertake this duty should wear some kind of identification. And what finer badge could they wear than the image of that most virtuous of all the women to whom this world ever gave birth, the Virgin Mary, with the child she had so miraculously conceived? They called in Father Zacharius of the Carmelites who approved the plan and designed a ribbon with a cross on it, at the centre of which was to be a picture of the Mother of God, as a symbol of virginity. The colours chosen were the papal colours of white and gold, to symbolise faith (besides which, no-one was going to call the virginity of the Pope in question). It was clear that the rescue of these girls should be carried out in a Roman Catholic spirit, with special emphasis on the benefits of piety. For surely even the most hardened pimp would give way before a virtuous maiden who was forever telling her beads, oblivious of all around her as she went about, continually whispering to herself and repeating one of those lovely litanies: 'From the spirit of fornication, Good Lord, deliver us!' And if on top of all that the maiden was old, hunchbacked and boss-eyed, she would not fall into the hands of the pimps, for she would be strengthened by her faith in eternal bliss and her pious beliefs would keep her safe from places of shame and moral depravity.

And so, when the Station Mission had been set up, Mrs Waldsteinová was singled out for the distinction of being the first who, armed with a ribbon from which it could be seen at first glance why this lady was spending so long walking about the station peering at everyone she met, set off to the rescue of innocent young girls who were arriving in Prague.

Two rooms had been made ready to receive them; furnished in modest style, it is true, but with a delicate understanding of the spiritual needs of innocent and inexperienced young girls from the country.

Everywhere she looked, such a girl would see the tortured face of the crucified Saviour staring back at her and even if she chanced to look up at the ceiling, there was a cross painted up there as well.

And between these crosses, which were to remind her that, if only for the sake of Him who had sacrificed Himself for her, she should maintain her innocence undefiled, there were inscriptions everywhere with the categorical imperative: 'Do not fornicate', though Countess Julia, ever the model of tact and good breeding, had in her innocence proposed that the legend should read: 'You are requested not to fornicate' or 'In the event of fornication, please contact the Director.'

Oh, the good, the innocent Countess Julia! The meaning of that word was as foreign to her as that of words like 'radioactivity' or

'Gautsch'* would be to a shepherd in the Appennines.

Mrs Waldsteinová walked about the station waiting for a train and when one at last arrived, she rushed full tilt at the first girl who came through the door carrying a suitcase. Her heart was boiling over with enthusiasm and she completely failed to notice that in the crush, her ribbon had fallen off her sleeve. Swiftly, she plucked the suitcase from the girl's hand but in that same instant, a policeman was on the scene and arrested her, and off they went to the police-station, followed by a large crowd.

In her confusion, she began to shout at first and then began to assert and explain that she was not a criminal, she was from the Station Mission. The further they went, the more confused she became and finally, only half-aware of what she was doing, she started to exhort the policeman to give up the life he was leading and stay away from the pimps.

It all got straightened out at the police-station but that did not prevent a certain journal, which took a very hostile attitude to the bourgeoisie, from coming out with an article headed: 'A Strange Case of Kleptomania'. A correction was published later, but the article left a stain. Mrs Waldsteinová withdrew from the Station Mission and the story goes that she invested the money she had inherited from her mother in a large brothel in Ustí nad Labem and is now making fifty per cent a year on the investment.

This setback in no way deterred the selfless ladies. On the contrary, it called forth among them such a readiness to sacrifice themselves for the good cause that Princess Boldierová herself descended on the station and came back in high triumph to the refuge with a girl in tow who took a lively interest in that philanthropic institution.

The ladies led her in procession into the refuge and instructed her till ten o'clock at night about the moral degradation that lay in wait in the city. And then the innocent Countess Julia took leave of the Station Mission's first victim with the words: 'I beg you from the bottom of my heart to refrain from fornicating!' The girl was given the keys to the place and told she could stay there until she had found herself a job.

She was there a week. For the first two days, she behaved respectably, but then she began to bring men back to this sanctified retreat of hers.

This was a terrible blow to Father Zacharius of the Carmelites when

* Karl, Freiherr von Gautsch, Prime Minister of the 'Austrian' part of the Empire, May–October 1911.

he called in early one morning to prepare her, during that idle hour of the day, for the approaching Easter Festival which means so much to the soul that burns with religious sensibility.

And it was frightful when to cap it all, the fellow threw the worthy Father out, which sad tidings of moral degeneracy he then relayed to the lady who was so earnestly fighting the good fight against immorality, the lofty-minded Princess Boldierová.

But who can know the depth of self-sacrificing ardour that fills the hearts of ladies such as this? Next to sally forth to the rescue of those girls at the station was Countess Solvarová and since that worthy lady was extremely short-sighted, she came back with some bent old crone to whom, as they rode along in the carriage, she kept saying: 'And you should thank God, young lady, that I have rescued you from the hands of the pimps!'

But why give up in despair over such an innocent mistake? The virtuous Countess Julia asked her mother's permission to go down to the station herself and meet the trains.

The noble, the innocent Countess! As she stood waiting for a train to come, she was approached by a smartly-dressed young man who showed a lively interest in the purpose of the ribbon she was wearing on her sleeve and in the aims of the Sacred Station Mission. The good Countess opened her virginal heart to him and he, young and elegant as he was, introduced himself to her as the Prince Godknowswhat. They had a most enjoyable conversation.

Poor innocent, young, virtuous Countess Julia! He bartered her, that hapless station missionary, that most innocent of innocent lilies, that chaste and virtuous flowerbud; he sold her for a hundred crowns, the blackguard, to a House of Ill Fame in Pilsen.

My pen is reluctant to proceed further, for the sad fate of the Station Mission is so deeply moving that one weeps in the act of writing, just as my friend Hájek is weeping now as he writes his employer's obituary.

1911

The Unfortunate Affair of the Tom-Cat

One day, during an argument with his neighbour Křička, Mr Hustoles said: 'A fine party, that party of yours! Any Tom, Dick or Harry straight from the gallows will do for it as a candidate!' To which Mr Křička said in reply: 'All right then, Mr Hustoles, we'll just wait and see, shall we?'

Not only was Mr Hustoles a deep political thinker, he was also the proud possessor of a large black tom-cat, which was usually to be found sitting on the threshold of his greengrocer's shop. This tom-cat was well-liked through the whole neighbourhood. It was a cat that the locals held in high esteem for its genial manner and light-hearted spirit which, as we all know, is half-way to good health. This cat was also respected for its affectionate nature and never in a million years would it have occurred to anyone to think that this excellent animal could acquire an enemy in the immediate vicinity.

Such an enemy arose, nevertheless, in the person of Mr Křička who said to his eight-year-old son Josef, after that political quarrel with Mr Hustoles:

'Pepíček, the next time you see the ugly black brute that belongs to that silly fool Hustoles, you tread on its tail!'

What child would not sally forth with a light heart on a secret mission of such gallantry?

Off Pepíček went and trod on the tom-cat's tail and he crowned his exploit by spitting all over the cat as well, a sight that made an old woman who saw it from across the street feel as if her heart would burst.

Then he ran off. For the first moment or two, the cat did not know quite what to think about all this but then, after giving the matter its most careful consideration, it came to the view that what that little blighter had done to it had hurt and that when he had blown water over it out of his mouth, it had felt unpleasant. By evening, it had come to the final conclusion that it had been insulted.

It made up its mind to watch out for the little ruffian.

Pepíček's father rewarded him for his valour with a kreutzer and promised him more if he would go on as he had begun for in Mr

Křička's eyes, the cat, being the property of his political adversary, stood for the whole of the enemy political party.

It was not just a tom-cat on whose tail Pepíček was treading in this case, it was the whole of the hostile political party and it wasn't just a cat he was spitting on, but each and every adherent of that party, among whom was numbered the owner of the cat in question.

Pepíček went gaily out to do battle in the political arena.

The tom-cat was sitting in front of the door and it looked to all the world as if it was sleeping. But all the world was deceived. That cat was only shamming. Let no-one condemn it for this behaviour: it did not go to school, so no-one had told it that it was a sin to pretend.

There is the cat, then, shamming away in the innocence of its heart and along comes Pepíček, treads on its tail and spits on its head.

But then, up jumps the cat and bites Pepíček in the leg.

And while it's at it, it spits, it clambers all over Pepíček, tears at him with its claws, hisses and growls, bites him in the ear for good measure, climbs down from him and with tail held high, walks away from the bawling youngster in a superior manner and sits calmly down on the threshold of its master's shop, purring demurely away.

When Pepíček arrived home, hoarse with crying and covered in blood, Mr Křička cried out: 'Praise be! Got you at last, Mr Hustoles!' and took his son off to the police-station, where the police doctor examined Pepíček and wrote a report on the whole case, whereupon the Police Commissar ordered that the cat be taken into custody and sent for veterinary examination.

So two policeman set off to bring the tom-cat in, and arrested it in the name of the law. And because it attempted to get away and scratched and spat, they had no option but to send for the municipal drunk-cart, into which they shut the cat, but not before it had rendered itself guilty of a public order offence by sinking its teeth into a police-uniform and laid itself open to the charge of contempt for the law by spitting at a policeman. What it had been growling under its breath, they had not been able to ascertain.

Then the cat was taken off to the veterinary section of the Agricultural Technical Science Department and the policemen submitted their report on its behaviour: 'When we arrived to apprehend the animal, it scratched and bit. We sent for the municipal drunk-cart and after a violent struggle, we threw it into the basket. It made an attempt to snatch one of our revolvers from us.'

This report was taken down, signed and submitted to the Public

Prosecutor's Office.

The Public Prosecutor decided that Mr Hustoles had been guilty of the offence of Failure to Exercise Sufficient Control Over An Animal.

He had not previously kept the cat on a chain, nor had he furnished it with a muzzle.

Next, this had occurred during an election, a time when an animal might easily contract rabies.

Further, political tension had existed for some considerable time between Mr Křička, the father of the party assaulted by the tom-cat, namely his son Josef, and Mr Hustoles, the owner of the black tom-cat that had committed the assault on the young lad belonging to Mr Křička. The Prosecutor's Office was therefore of the opinion that a case had been established against the cat owned by Mr Hustoles, to wit that it had with malice aforethought set out to occasion grievous bodily harm to the young son of its master's political adversary, in which intention it had been successful and which act it had carried out. But since, according to the relevant Austrian law of 8th January 1801, cats were classified as persons of diminished mental responsibility, for whom the owners were required to answer with their names and their lives, the guilt fell exclusively on Mr Hustoles.

The veterinary institute attached to the Agricultural Technical Science Department had meanwhile carried out an examination of the cat's physical and mental condition and the papers had been sent on to the Prosecutor's Office.

The medical report ran as follows:

Mr František Hustoles

The subject was found to have strong bones and to be in a well-nourished condition, but to be suffering from periostitis, so that its bite could constitute a danger to life.

For these reasons, it is desirable that the subject be put down.

Dr M. Kašpárek

The Public Prosecutor's Office sent this document to the police-station for action and it was immediately filed with the papers on the Hustoles case.

The cat, meanwhile, had been returned to Hustoles and great was the surprise of the wretched man's family when at five o'clock one morning, four policemen arrived to pick Mr Hustoles up, and took the unfortunate man away. At the police-station, a stern-faced sergeant asked the prisoner none too gently:

'Are you František Hustoles?'

'Yes Sir, I am, Sir.'

Tears began to glisten in the eyes of a young policeman in the corner.

'Bring me the papers relating to František Hustoles and don't blubber!'

The papers were brought.

'I shall now read out to you, Hustoles, Gubernatorial Decree No. 75–289, dated 15th June, 1911:

In the matter of František Hustoles, it has been decided, on the basis of Veterinary Report No. 2145/65, that the said person be put down without delay. On the basis of para. 5 of the law relating to rinderpest of 12th February 1867, there is no appeal against this decision.

Signed

Vaníček
Councillor, Imperial and Royal Prosecutor's Office

'As you see,' the sergeant said to the unhappy man, 'there is no appeal. Make your final dispositions and stop bawling. You're going to be put down one way or another, as soon as Vienna confirms the sentence and informs us of the method to be used.'

I'm really curious to know how Mr Hustoles managed to get himself out of that one.

1911

An Incident that occurred during Minister Trnka's Tour of Inspection

The best possible proof that the loyal Austrian patriotism of the Czech people has not been lost is afforded by Minister Trnka's tour of inspection. They did the Minister pretty well on that tour. As he himself says, he consumed twenty-eight geese, forty-six ducks, fifteen hares and a hundred and twenty partridges. And to follow the geese, ducks, hares and partridges, his hosts had served him up a series of scrolls making him an honorary citizen of their respective towns.

Truly, it was a triumphal progress. Everywhere, banners in the Habsburg colours of black and gold had fluttered out to greet him.

Maids of honour, priests, firemen, mayors; all had trembled and stuttered as they addressed him, or he them.

And so he travelled on from one inn to the next, his officials drew up maps and schedules, and everywhere he made notes, as for example: 'Pardubice: mayonnaise. The eggs should have been fresher.'

And then one day – whoosh! His car went up in flames in Mladá Boleslav and all his schedules, maps and notes with it, and all that was left to the Minister were his memories of those good Czech folk and their patriotic loyalty, memories that raised many a chuckle in the ministerial soul. Such as, for example, the memory of Štěchovice.

A Minister of the government is a great sensation for Štěchovice. Until that time, there was not a single Štěchovician who had ever seen a minister, much less spoken to one.

Picture them now, then, entrusting the village schoolmaster with the task of standing in a punt and pronouncing an Address of Welcome as the Minister arrived.

The Štěchovicians are sticklers for ceremony where Distinguished Visitors are concerned. They resolved that the teacher would have to greet the Minister with an address composed in verse.

The schoolmaster sweated buckets. He climbed every hill in the vicinity, seeking out the most beautiful and secluded spot available, so that he might devote himself in peace to the task of poetic composition.

At last, it is said, he found a cave in the Bojanov valley. And to that cave, for three days, they sent his food and drink by the hand of the village policeman.

And in these three days he gave birth to the following Address:

> Your Excellency's boat most ardently we hail,
> As o'er the stream from Svatý Jan you sail;
> May your face shine, Your Worship, with good cheer,
> All Štěchovice waits, Your Lordship, for you here.

The great day arrived. He had had these lines written out on a piece of fine paper, had put on his best dark suit and a top hat, and now he stood there, this glorious bard, perched on the edge of the punt and his face pale with expectation, strained longing eyes in the direction from which the ministerial boat was to come.

And here it came and the mortars boomed and the eyes of the whole community turned and fixed themselves on their bard.

As the Minister's boat was laying up alongside the punt, the latter pitched and the schoolmaster went flying. And there he was swimming around in the water, eyes bulging and calling out to the Minister: 'Please don't be angry, Your Excellency, the water's nice and warm!'

1912

Brief Outline of a Blood-and-Thunder Romance

'Giuseppe Boro has arrived in Terst. Not having enough money for a long stay, he has introduced himself to the innkeeper Bittornelli as Count Ulrich von Eisenfels. The innkeeper's beautiful daughter Lucia falls in love with the fake Count, but Giuseppe Boro is being watched by Lorenzo, a villainous sailor from that town, who knows certain secrets from Boro's past, namely that in Rome, he killed the man who had seduced his sister, along with three other men who had aided and abetted the seducer. Greatly alarmed by this, Giuseppe Boro confides in Bittornelli, the two having drunk wine together and become bosom friends. The pair decide to poison Lorenzo, invite him round for a drink and put their plan successfully into operation. But since there is a great deal of work involved in getting rid of a body, they let the innkeeper's daughter Lucia into the secret as well. They put Lorenzo's body in a sack and carry it off at night into the mountains behind the town, where there are deep chasms. The plan is to throw the bag into one of these chasms and they are poised over just such a sheer drop when a gendarme takes them by surprise. Lucia comes to the rescue by plunging a dagger into the gendarme's heart at the very moment when he has just leapt down from his horse to see what all the commotion is about. They throw the bodies of Lorenzo and the gendarme into the chasm but as they are doing this, the riderless horse whinnies, they hear the thud of horses' hooves close by and a fresh gendarme appears on the scene. Giuseppe Boro shoots this one down with his pistol and they all go quietly off home. That's as far as I've got, Mr Toms.'

As he sat opposite Mr Toms, the publisher of blood-and-thunder romances, the young man looked sadly into the eyes of that kindly soul, who exclaimed: 'But this really is beyond a joke, Mr Krámský! What comes next? Where are you going to put all the other bodies? Your people should stay where they are, because the shot is bound to bring yet another gendarme patrol on the scene. It's a life-and-death struggle – that's how I see it – you wring the man's neck . . . do you understand what I'm saying, young man?

'And by the way, you're very careless in your use of firearms. You let off a gun at night, when you're carrying a corpse off to throw it down a cliff, and when you've already killed one gendarme. That's a mistake, a big mistake: you're giving yourself clear away. If that Lucia of yours is so handy with a knife, why not stab the other gendarme as well?'

Mr Toms rose to his feet and leaning on a table in the half-full coffee-house shouted aloud in the passion of his argument: 'Why, I ask you yet again, did you not kill that second gendarme with a dagger? You could have shoved a dagger into his heart as well and that would have been an end of the whole charade.

'As sure as eggs is eggs, young man, you just can't go on working with the old tried-and-trusted formulae. That's the youth of today for you! You ought to have known Charvát – he's dead now – he knew a thing or two about how to handle a dagger! That was in 1900 and he went on till 1905 – in Germany, it was – and he worked only with daggers and poison. Shooting at night creates a racket and if you go on like that, then I'd be grateful if you'd explain to me how you're going to get yourself out of trouble: you'll land yourself in a terrible mess!

'I'm talking to you like a father. You're quick on the uptake and I reckon that this isn't a complete write-off. What you've got to do now is seize your chance of making a getaway. Don't you see, it's just not on to go back to town after what has happened. Hit the road into the wide world. You'll have to start out as a robber. You kill some women and children and you get that Lucia female locked up and then you rescue her. You make your way, if necessary, to where she is being held and you overpower the guards. That's the main thing. I'd recommend a rubber cosh: certainly not a revolver, because a shot would raise the alarm and you'd be back in trouble again.'

'You have my word for it that there'll be no shooting,' answered the young man. 'I'm grateful for your advice. But can I go on using poison? Which poisons work without leaving a trace?'

'It's easy to see that you've not had the experience in the field that the late Charvát had. All poisons leave traces and then there's a post-mortem. Just let there be a post-mortem and the doctors will find strychnine, for instance. If you use poison, you should really go to town. Poison rich relatives in particular, and people like that. And do it slowly: you get the best results that way.

'But before I forget, it'll be all right after you've killed the guards. And remember, in this day and age you're expected to rob every bank in sight. You knock out the attendants with chloroform or creep up on them surreptitiously and inject curare into their bloodstream. A heavy iron safe, you blow it with dynamite. And then you *can* use revolvers. A revolver is fine on a bank-job; a Browning is a nice little number. A train-robbery would make a nice splash as well. And you can raid public places, too: theatres, restaurants, coffee-houses. And if anyone resists and refuses to hand over the money, then you shoot him down in cold blood like a dog – like a dog, I say! And now, young man, off you go and get cracking!'

They got up and found to their surprise that they were surrounded by a circle made up of the customers, the waiter, the waiter's assistant and the proprietor of the coffee-house: all kneeling in an attitude of mute resignation to their fate and raising their clasped hands in a plea for mercy.

1912

Human Vanity

My experience as a local reporter has given me occasion to marvel at
the vanity of which human beings are capable . . .

It chanced one day I wrote that a certain gentleman from Smíchov
by the name of Václav Stránský had got himself so pickled in a bar on
Kinský Avenue that he had been thrown out of the establishment in
front of a large crowd of onlookers and that his hat had been crushed in
the process. Next day, Mr Václav Stránský appeared in the office in a
state of high excitement and asked me to correct the story to the effect
that it had been a *top*-hat of his, not just any old tuppeny-ha'penny hat,
that had been damaged.

A few days later, another case occurred, and the cause this time was
a story in which I described how a fire had been put out in the
pork-butcher's shop of a Mr Slabý.

It had, I wrote, been a truly dangerous fire, for the flour in the
sausages had gone up with elemental force. I wrote this with the best of
intentions, namely to entertain the reader, for I regarded it as the
sacred duty of a local reporter never to be dull.

Next day, three people came to the office, Mr Slabý the pork-
butcher, his father and his grandfather.

The most belligerent of the three was the old gentleman who kept
egging his son and grandson on to give me a going-over, while the
grandson said in a voice pregnant with emotion: 'If only you were to
taste our bangers' and the son kept bawling that I had ruined his trade.

Just as things were reaching a critical stage, in came the Editor-in-
Chief and I judged it to be the most tactically sound policy that I
should now disappear, after stammering that they should take it up
with the responsible editor.

The word 'responsible' had no sooner fallen from my lips than it
exercised such a charm on our visitors that they started to pull my chief
about like children playing with a puppy and when he eventually got
away from them, they ran after him into the printing-room and when
he finally barricaded himself into the smallest room of all, they
hammered on the door and tried to batter it in, like a mob in a

cholera-epidemic. It was the grandfather, again, whose behaviour was
the most uncivilised. He banged on the door and roared: 'We'll give
you a bellyful of those floury bangers!'

'Gentlemen,' piped the Editor in his reedy voice, 'It's not my fault.
We got the story from the police and it went into the paper without my
knowledge.'

All of my readers, I am sure, know how often an Editor gets blamed
by those stern judges among the public for something arising out of a
lack of due care and attention in the office . . . and these three men
were behaving worse than a Mexican jury.

It was only when the workmen on the staff came running up that the
clan of butchers could be removed from the building by force,
whereupon they went off to sort it out with the police.

And so later on, when I went to the police-station to check on some
stories relating to broken legs, suicides and vicious cats, a collision
somewhere involving an electric tram and some theft or other, the
Chief Commissar met me with the request that I refrain henceforth
from landing him with any more pork-butchers whose floury sausages
had gone up in flames.

The epilogue of this affair was played out in the daily paper
published by our political opponents, to which the butcher-family had
turned for help. They came out against us with a piece of purple prose
on the bankruptcy of our party's trade-policy. The whole article rested
on the high moral argument that we were the paid lackeys of big
business, intent on grinding the small trader into the dust. The day
would come, it concluded, when our party would be swept from the
face of the earth, lock, stock and barrel.

So I resolved that I would no longer report the local news in such a
spectacular manner, but with dry, precise objectivity.

And so I wrote: 'At five o'clock yesterday afternoon, Jan Kysela, a
cabinet-maker, quarrelled with his wife Maria, *née* Fochtová, in his
workshop at 612 Žižkov, and hit her on the head with an iron bar, so
that she had to be taken to hospital by a vehicle from the emergency
service. The occurrence caused a large crowd to collect.'

When I arrived at the office next day, the attendant met me on the
stairs with a worried expression on his face and told me that there were
two men waiting for me in the office. They had already sat down and
one of them had a big thick stick in his hand.

Without any preliminaries, he addressed me in an angry voice: 'Mr
Editor, is this an iron bar?'

I had to concede him this point. No, I declared, he was not mistaken; this was indeed not an iron bar.

'So you see,' he went on in a calmer tone, 'I only hit her on the head with this bit of wood here' and he went on to speak with feeling of the fact that he would certainly never have been capable of such brutality as to hit his wife with an iron bar.

And then, how could he, as a cabinet-maker, have had an iron bar handy? By the time he had found one, the anger would have passed.

So it was no more than the performance of a pleasant duty when, in the interests of justice, I corrected that report.

'It is not true,' I wrote, 'that cabinet-maker Jan Kysela from Žižkov struck his wife with an iron bar. Mr Kysela came into our office yesterday with a large stick two metres and forty centimetres in length and informed us that it was with this stick alone and in no way with an iron bar that he had beaten his wife over the head.'

I did not expect that this man, whom I had so handsomely vindicated in the eyes of the public, would come back to the office with that same stick and beat me over the head as well, explaining as he did so that he was acting in this way solely because I had given the affair undue extra publicity. Yes indeed, such is the vanity of the human race!

Once, we got a visit from Alfonso the Dwarf, who came in the company of his impresario Massarini, because he was currently on show in Prague for an entrance-fee of forty hellers a time.

I wrote a gripping article about him, portraying him as the most hideous monster on earth, one that the paying customers would find a delight to behold. His impresario had this translated and somehow, a misunderstanding crept in. He got the impression that he was the hideous creature that I had been describing.

And he shot me three times with his revolver, rejoicing in this opportunity to defend his reputation for manly beauty with so much *éclat*.

From that day forth, since one of his bullets wounded me in the shoulder, I have been unable to write any more articles, to the great delight, no doubt, of all our readers.

1912

Mr Florentin *vs.* Chocholka

Mr Florentin was a class-teacher and Chocholka was a first-former. Mr Florentin was Chocholka's class-teacher and he was also the Latin master, while Latin, for Chocholka, was a struggle of naked brutality. Latin made him think of Spain and it was not a castle of which he thought, but a boot: the Spanish Boot which was put to such good use, in the days of the Inquisition, to the greater glory of God. Mr Florentin would look down with a disdain to equal that of the Inquisition at the face of first-former Chocholka as he sat there aghast, shaking his way through the whole of the Latin lesson and literally shaking out the first and second declensions. And when the hour of the third declension had come, Chocholka's shaking transformed itself into a veritable fever. And then, whenever Mr Florentin glanced at him, Chocholka would lift his stupefied eyes to the ceiling and ask permission to leave the room. He would go out in the same way when his turn to answer a question was coming round. And when the time arrived for the written examinations, Chocholka trembled in abject fear, wondering how he could possibly survive the Latin.

It was the day of the first Latin test and there sat Chocholka – prayers having been said and exercise-books given out with the warning that there was to be no copying and that any pupils found to have made identical mistakes would be failed outright – there was Chocholka, taking his pen in his quivering fingers and copying down from the blackboard the sentences which he was to translate into Latin. He had one thought in mind: he had to make different mistakes from those of his neighbour or he'd be failed outright and that would be the end of him. He wrote down the first word of his rough version and stole a sly glance sideways at his neighbour Batĕk, who also had the reputation of being anything but a star performer. That glance at his neighbour's work was enough to convince him finally that he and Batĕk were both doomed. For Batĕk had begun his version in exactly the same way that he had. Chocholka took fright and his tearful gaze slid from the depressing picture of the ruins of Troy on the wall down to the instrument of salvation, the key to the latrines. And just as in

Hellenic times a criminal on the run would seek refuge in some place of
sanctuary, so Chocholka grabbed the key and legged it for the latrines,
turning his back on Classical civilisation, which shone forth on the
blackboard in sentences like: 'The table is neither high nor wide; The
heel is a part of the body; A foot-soldier is a warrior; A mother is not a
sister; In Rome there were many houses; In the garden there are
trees' . . . and other such profound truths.

All this he left behind him. His only thought was to hold out in the
toilet, the hiding-place, the refuge for all first-formers who were heated
in the chase, until the end of the lesson, so that his written exercise
should be a shining example of linguistic chastity, a void in which not a
single offence against either the grammar or the spirit of the Latin
language could be found. And when the absent-minded teacher
questioned him as to why he had not done his translation, he would
reply without turning a hair: 'Please, Sir, I was on the toilet for the
whole lesson.' And if they didn't believe him, he would take them to
the place and then they would see written on a panel the words:
'Václav Chocholka, IA, 16.xi.' And he wrote this inscription on the
wall in bold characters and sat locked inside that tiny enclosure, not
exactly in a calm state of mind, but certainly more or less resigned to
whatever fate might befall him.

Someone came running down the corridor, banged on the door and
called out: 'Chocholka, you've got to get a move on!' 'I can't,' came
Chocholka's reply to Mr Florentin's message. While Messenger
Fourteen dashed back so as not to miss too much of his examination,
Chocholka sat on in the full and solemn realisation that with those two
words: 'I can't', he had defied the authority of his class-teacher. War
had been declared. Five minutes later, Messenger Fourteen was back
again, knocking on the door of Chocholka's last resort. 'You really
have got to get on with it!' 'I can't,' answered Chocholka once more,
but this time in a tone as proud as that with which Leonidas had
answered the Persian envoys at Thermopylae. Peace descended once
again on the gloomy school corridor where every footstep resounded
with a loud echo. Chocholka was counting the seconds and minutes
and he had got almost up to six hundred, which meant that it was
about ten minutes since the last communication from Mr Florentin.

Then came the ring of determined footsteps and Chocholka was
startled by a heavy pounding on the door. 'Chocholka, come out now,
or you'll never get your composition finished.'

'I can't, Sir!' came the quivering, timid voice of Chocholka.

'I order you to come out!' A fierce struggle arose in Chocholka's soul in which the spirit of mutiny was victorious.

'I'm sorry, Sir,' he said, this time in a firm tone, 'I can't.'

'You won't come out, then?'

'I'm sorry, I can't.'

Mr Florentin ran off to the Headmaster's study. 'Headmaster, one of my pupils, a boy called Chocholka, is spending the time allotted for his first written test on the toilet and he won't vacate it.'

The Headmaster rose, his eyes blazing with anger at such depravity, and the two of them advanced with determined tread on Chocholka's retreat.

Mr Florentin knocked first. 'Chocholka, pull yourself together! The Headmaster is here. Come out of the toilet.'

'Look here, Chocholka, you come on out!' said the Headmaster, making his presence felt. 'Don't be disobedient, or you'll regret it. Where do you live?'

'Number Five, Army Street, Headmaster,' the class-teacher informed him. 'His mother is a charwoman.'

'Now come on, Chocholka,' said the Headmaster reproachfully. 'Your mother goes out to work and instead of bringing joy to the poor woman's heart by getting yourself a good mark in your Latin composition, you just sit there on the toilet and you won't budge. Don't you feel at all sorry for your mother? But what's the point of all this talking? I order you to come out and return to your duties!'

'I can't, not yet.'

'Don't try to make fools of us! You'll have your name put in the punishment book!'

'I can't!'

'You'll lose marks for conduct!'

'Can't!'

'You'll be expelled from school!'

'Can't!!'

Mass psychology works in a mysterious way. The class-teacher's eyes flashed. The Headmaster gave a roar like a rutting stag and the two worthy gentlemen hurled their combined weight against the door of the toilet. It was a fearsome onslaught and Chocholka, hearing their efforts to force their way in, braced himself against the door with all his strength, in an attempt to hold the pass. But his efforts were in vain. From outside, Mr Florentin and the Headmaster rammed the full force of their bodies against the gates of the fortress, the gates gave way, and they burst into the interior.

But the fortress was empty. Hearing the rending of the door and resolved not to be taken alive and forced to do his composition, Chocholka had plunged head first into the toilet.

'It's better for him this way,' said Mr Florentin. 'He'd have made a terrible hash of the composition.'

But the Headmaster called down into the last ditch which had swallowed up its doughty defender: 'Chocholka, you're to stay in after school for six hours!'

1912

The Austrian Customs

I was on an excursion to Dresden and one day, as ill-luck would have it, I was rambling about in the environs of the city when I got run over by an express train. I was so thoroughly mangled that it took them a year and a half to put me properly together again. I had planned to return to Prague from my Dresden trip in four days, but it took more than eighteen months.

We are all in God's hands, of course, but I had been in the hands of the doctors as well.

I was a fearsome sight. To this day, I don't know how much of me was mine. All I do know is that I had been artificially reassembled by eighteen doctors and fifty-two assistants. And a fine job they had made of it. I was given a certificate detailing the parts from which I had been reconstituted, so that I would qualify for support as an invalid, and that certificate was fourteen pages long.

The only bits of me that remained were a segment of brain, some part of my stomach, approximately fifteen kilograms of my own flesh and half a litre of my own blood. All the other parts were foreign, except that they had stitched the heart together out of some bits of my own and some from an ox. I was a real triumph of medical science.

Externally, I was totally artificial, as the certificate also made clear. It was a fine example of the miraculous power of medicine to construct a new man out of a variety of parts, like a child making a castle out of building-blocks.

When I was discharged, I went to the Central Cemetery to visit the last resting-place of my remains in the section where they sent human parts from the hospital for burial, and then I made my way to the station and set off for Prague knowing that I had perhaps got more out of my visit to Dresden than any other tourist who had ever come to that beautiful city.

In Děčín, we had to submit to examination by the Austrian Customs. After they had hauled out our luggage and ferreted about in it for a while, the eye of one Customs official fell on me. That special look I had of a man who had been artificially put together seemed to have aroused in this official the impression that someone who looked like that must at the very least be trying to get saccharine through the Customs. I had the look of a really hard-bitten smuggler.

'Let's have your case over here,' the man said to me, 'and you come along with me to the office.' In the office they opened my case, searched it and found nothing suspicious, until they noticed among my papers the certificate that had been issued by the hospital in Dresden and signed by eighteen professors of medicine and fifty-two assistants.

'Good Heavens!' they said to me after they had had a look at the certificate. 'You'll have to go and see the Chief. You can't enter Austria in this state.'

A model of rectitude the Chief Customs Officer is, a man acutely aware of his responsibilities. After examining the certificate, he said: 'First of all, according to this certificate, you've got a silver plate in place of the back of your skull. That silver isn't hallmarked and that means that you pay a fine of twelve crowns. There's a hundred and twenty grams of that silver and according to sections VI and VIII (b) of paragraph 946 of Customs Regulations (knowingly attempting to smuggle unhallmarked silver), that's a triple fine. Three times twelve, that's thirty-six crowns.

'Next, the duty on a hundred and twenty grams of silver (sections (b) and (f)/(g) on the Schedule of the International Convention of 1902) is ten hellers per gram, so a hundred and twenty grams makes twelve crowns. Then you've got a horse's bone in place of your left femur. We shall have to classify that as importation of an undeclared bone. And that, my friend, is a stab in the back for the Austrian animal-bone industry.

'For what purpose are you walking about with a foreign horse's bone inside you? So that you can walk? Right, we'll put that down as employment of a horse-bone in pursuance of trade. We'll have the truth out of you, my fine friend!

'Pursuance of trade is all very well, but it won't get you anywhere, because we have a heavy duty on failure to report animal-bones imported into Austria. That'll cost you twenty crowns.

'And then there's a note here that you've had three ribs replaced with platinum wire. Good grief, man! You're bringing platinum into Austria? Do you know what you've got coming to you? Three hundred times the normal fine! Let's see, now: if those three bits of wire weigh twenty grams, that comes to 1,605 crowns. You've really been wickedly irresponsible.

'But what's this I see?

'It says here that part of your kidneys, the left one to be exact, has been replaced by a pig's kidney.

'My dear sir! The importation of pigs into Austria is prohibited. And that applies to parts of pigs as well. So if you want to enter Bohemia, that kidney has got to stay in Germany.'

And since I wouldn't agree to that, I've been hanging about in Saxony for ten years now, waiting for the Agrarian Party (I'm an Agrarian voter) to permit the importation of pigs into Austria. Then I'll return to my native land.

1912

The Demon Barber of Prague

(A Tragedy in One Act)

(The barber, Mr Špachta, is in full flow. His victim has been thoroughly soaped and Mr Špachta has set about shaving him with all due ceremony. He chats to his customer as he works)

'So now the Turks are in for it at last. Those Turkish so-and-so's have pushed further and further and at last the Eyeties have said: "That's far enough!" Head right back, Your Honour, if you would be so kind. We old soldiers, Your Honour . . . it's just a little scratch, Your Honour: the lazy devil has forgotten to soap that little bristly bit there. Head back, Your Honour, that's it . . . We old soldiers know a thing or two about war. The Eyeties are very well armed, Your Honour and the Turks won't want to be far behind. I just hope Serbia doesn't get involved, Your Honour; it's all boiling up just now, down in the Balkans. It was nothing, Your Honour, just a wart. The thing to do with them is to cut them off with the razor and they won't grow again. The Great Powers won't like it, Your Honour. It's a powder-keg, the Balkans; all of a sudden, it can go off "Bang!" No, no, Your Honour, the skin's not broken; it was just one of those little pimples. You're much better nipping them off than squeezing them out. And you see, Your Honour, perhaps the Hungarians will open the border and let the Serbian cattle in, just so as the Serbs don't sell them to the Turkish army. But they won't do that. The best thing would be if the Turks died of hunger, but if they can't manage that, they'll drive the camels after the army. That's the way I see it, Your Honour. You've got to play it canny with the Turks. They're a fly lot, them Turks: they've given up Tripoli now, but they'll withdraw into the interior and get together with the Arabs and start a guerilla war, and then there'll be some cut and thrust – oh no, Sir, that wasn't a cut, just some little insect: can't leave that there. It'll be tough, Your Honour, a guerilla war like that; a lot of blood will flow. Oh no, Your Honour, you mustn't think that, it wasn't part of the lip, just a little bit of a cold-sore that I've shaved off and that's a very good thing, Sir, believe me. You must have had a bit of a scare during the night, Your Worship, and who wouldn't feel scared these days? And if war breaks out right across Europe, there'll be cold-sores appearing all over the place and it will be terrible, Your Honour: brothers will be butchering each other . . . don't worry, Your Honour, just a slip of the razor, we'll soon stop the bleeding . . . there! all back to normal again! If only the Great Powers could say that, eh? I don't know what's got into this razor today, Your Honour; it's as if it wanted to go and fight against the Turks. Like quicksilver it is, and sharp with it. Believe me, Your Honour, if I didn't have a family, I'd be off to fight the Turks myself. And that's not because they're unbelievers. Nobody gives a monkey's about that nowadays, you can believe what you like. It's because they're Turks. They're filth, them Turks; just look at the Turks in Prague, Your Honour, look at the trousers they wear: it's enough to give you the shivers. And then, when instead of the knicknacks they sell, they stick a long knife into their belt and then a short one and then a pistol and then another pistol and one of those *khanjars*, those swords of theirs and you bump into one and he comes at you with all that lot . . . Your Honour, Your Honour, it's only a little piece of skin gone; just got to finish shaving that bit. It's no fun and games tangling with Turks; they're like dragons, the lot of them. And the Eyeties are like wild men: God help them all when the balloon goes up! It'll be a right dust-up, Your Honour. Oh my God! We'll soon put it right, Your Honour, believe me, it was only another of them beasties. It had to come off, Your Honour, there was nothing I could do but cut it away. Oh, and did you hear, Your Honour, that the Turks have cut the Eyeties off from the sea around Tripoli? They're sending the *bashibazuks* in; a right gang, they are . . . Just turn your head sideways, Your Honour, we're just going to shave under the nose now. Well, Your Honour, the Eyeties aren't hanging back either; they're sending in one regiment after another. But the Arabs, Your Honour, they're joining up with the Turks; they have the same religion and they're glad of the chance of a slash and a stab . . . For Heaven's sake, Your Honour, don't faint on me! Josef, just sprinkle some water on the gentleman and wipe the blood away from his nose . . . There now, Your Honour, everything's all right again. It wasn't the tip of your nose, just a wart. You had a wart on the end of your nose, Sir, a birthmark perhaps, and that had to go. Why, it was disfiguring Your Honour's face. Oh, and I mustn't forget: the Eyeties will have their hands full against the Turks when the

Arabs have risen against the Rumanians. The Arab, Your Honour, is a worse bastard than the Turk in my opinion; cut off your head, he will . . . Josef, give the gentleman a sprinkle! It's nothing, Your Honour, just a bit of skin, just a bit off the top. Skin's a nuisance when it won't give, so off with it, I say! I'll run off to Tripoli, on my soul I will! There now, Your Honour. Josef, bring some water! Now then, Your Honour, I'm going to give you a good wash, and then shave over again. No, really, Your Honour, I've got to, you've got to be done again . . . give me that new razor, Josef! What do you think, Your Honour . . . head well back now . . . who'd have thought the blood would start to flow again? No, Your Honour, I just caught that old wound; I'm very careful, I don't want any dissatisfied customers . . . you know, Your Honour, the whole world's turned upside down today. It doesn't matter where you look; there's rebellion everywhere and there'll be blood flowing before long and Great God in Heaven, Your Honour! Bring him round, Josef! The nose is intact, Your Honour, it was just the bit under the nose, only a tiny bit, hardly worth mentioning. Oh, what a lovely war there'd be if those Turks would just start the ball rolling! It's got me all in a tizzy, Your Honour. Josef, give me that bandage! It'll soon pass, Your Honour, cuts soon heal over; there, Your Honour, we'll just put a sticking-plaster on and now, if you wouldn't mind turning your head round so that we can shave it clean on that side as well . . . You know, Your Honour, man's a bloodthirsty beast! There'll be orphans and lamentations and weeping when the news comes in from the battlefield. Josef, wrap that ear up in a bit of paper . . . All right again now, Your Honour, you gave me a fright when you fell off the chair. Like a meteor, you were; soon have you right again. They say that meteors have started falling again; that means a war, Your Honour, it's a sure sign, an age-old sign. Right, then, Your Honour, we'll just finish you off under the chin . . . No, no, Your Honour, it's got to be done, please don't shift about like that! It's a terrible thing, war, especially in a savage land like Africa. Just do you under the chin now, Your Honour, soon be all over. Do you know, Your Honour, that those wild men down there cut their prisoners' throats? First, they catch their prisoner and then they take a long knife and they put it under his chin, just like that . . . just a little bit longer, Your Honour, nearly done now . . . just like that, Your Honour, and Snap! Off with his head! Josef, pick up that head and put it away somewhere . . .

(Pause)

'Oh my Good Gawd, Your Honour, what have you gone and done?'

(Mr Špachta falls in a dead faint)

1912

Mr Čaboun: the Making of a Hooligan

You will, I am sure, have had the experience of being called rude names. You leave home bright and early one day, firmly convinced you're as decent a person as ever walked the earth, and there lying in wait for you is a beggar, a grizzled old codger, and when you give him a heller, he flings it down at your feet and starts to shout: 'You no-good bloody layabout!' So very early on, you know you're a layabout and as the morning progresses, you find out you're a sodding great brute. Of this you are informed by the old lady in the tram whose foot you have stood on. Then nothing gives you pleasure any more; you go back home and in the entrance, you collide with a man who's carrying something extremely hard wrapped up in a parcel. He crashes into you with it, so hard it takes your breath away and then he says: 'Can't you look where you're going, you stupid dozy bugger?' You think of making some remark, the man deposits his parcel on the ground and you feel it might be better to melt quietly away into the house and back into your flat. You got up in the morning thinking you were quite someone and you come home at midday a no-good bloody layabout, a sodding great brute and a stupid dozy bugger.

Nothing of this sort had ever happened to Mr František Čaboun. Never had this gentleman had a cross word addressed to him. And a very worthy gentleman he was; a retired librarian, formerly in the employ of a prince. This nice old buffer was scented through and through, as if with musk, with humanistic culture, in which he had become steeped as he arranged the prince's medieval manuscripts in the library and the sonorous Latin verses had permeated his mentality. His manner was courtesy itself: 'You were kind enough to enquire?' and 'Please allow me, I beg.' He was also very fond of flowers and the fuchsias outside his window enjoyed his comprehensive and tender care.

One fine day, he was watering his blooms and as ill-luck would have it, a sunbeam tickled his nose as he was gazing up into the blue sky. He sneezed, and the watering-can in his hand began to jump about as if there had been an earthquake, shedding some of its contents down onto the pavement. He looked out in alarm from behind the curtains at a gentleman with a big black moustache, who was standing there on the pavement wiping drops of water off his coat and shouting: 'Hooliganism, that's what it is, pure hooliganism!' To which another voice replied: 'That's it exactly, hooliganism.'

Mr František Čaboun stood there trembling behind the curtains and then tiptoed off to his bedroom, got undressed, put the watering-can away in a cupboard and got into bed, even though it was a lovely day.

Once in bed, he burst out in lamentation: 'So I'm a hooligan then! A hooligan in my declining years! I who have always lived by the book!' When he closed his eyes, he heard that sharp voice saying: 'Hooliganism, that's what it is!'

For the first time in his life, someone had called him names. His head swam with the shock and when evening came, he sat down at his desk and covered sheet after sheet of paper. Next afternoon, this letter arrived in the office of every daily paper in Prague, containing the declaration of Mr František Čaboun:

To the Editor,

Dear Sir,

I would most respectfully request, in the interest of removing a stain on my honour, the courtesy of your most esteemed columns so that I might give my account of an occurrence shortly before four o'clock yesterday afternoon, in Carmelite Street. I am a passionate lover of fuchsias and as I was watering them, I sneezed, thereby inadvertently sprinkling a little water on a certain gentleman with a black moustache who happened to be passing at just that moment. This unfortunate incident was erroneously interpreted as 'Hooliganism'. I am a man of advanced years, a retired librarian formerly in the employ of a Prince, and I am sure the public will realise that I am not the kind of person who would deliberately pour water on anyone from my window. Never in my life have I performed a mischievous action and I am certainly very far from feeling the inclination to sprinkle anyone. I trust that you, Sir, will see fit to accommodate this explanation of mine in your journal and would like to offer you my thanks in advance.

Yours Faithfully,
František Čaboun,
(Princely Librarian; retd.)

In their various offices, the editors looked at each other with a meaning expression, touched their foreheads and said: 'Persecution mania'.

When they duly omitted to publish his letter, he was devastated and pondered as to how he could yet clear his name before the public.

Then he took out an advertisement in all the papers: 'I would be most grateful if the gentleman who was sprinkled in error on Thursday 15 September would come to 27 Carmelite Street, so that we might become more closely acquainted. František Čaboun, Princely Librarian (retd.).'

Nobody came. All he got was an anonymous letter which ran: 'Now I can see what a hooligan you are, since you want to make fun of me as well!'

'If only I could meet the gentleman I sprinkled,' sighed Mr Čaboun despondently, 'everything would be all right. I'd be able to give him a satisfactory explanation and my name would be cleared. What sort of hooligan could I possibly be?'

He couldn't get it off his mind. At last he could contain himself no longer and confronted the concierge direct: 'What do you think? Am I a hooligan?'

'Good Heavens, Sir,' cried that worthy lady. 'Your Honour is such a nice gentleman!'

His mind at rest, he returned to his dwelling full of a sense of well-being. Those words had comforted him and he took his watering-can and went to water his fuchsias.

As he was on the point of sprinkling them, he saw walking along the pavement below that gentleman with the black moustache, that very same sprinkled citizen who had so insidiously haunted his dreams.

'Please allow me, I beg,' he called down, in the joyous hope that all would now be cleared up.

But the man with the black moustache walked on as if he had heard nothing.

Just as he was, Mr František Čaboun rushed through the door and down the stairs to the street.

In his shirt and underpants and grasping a watering-can.

He flew out through the main gate and ran up to the man with the black moustache, calling: 'Mr Sprinkled Gentleman, Sir, please allow me, I beg!'

The man thus addressed twisted round, saw the panting countenance of Mr Čaboun and the watering-can in his hand and thought: 'My

God, he wants to throw water over me again!' And took to his heels.
After him ran Mr Čaboun, calling out: 'Please allow me . . .'

There was a policeman standing at the corner and the man with the
black moustache fled to his protective wing like a chick to a mother-
hen. And so Mr Čaboun, in full flight, ran into the policeman and on
impact, the watering-can shed its contents over the tunic of this grave
personage. Next day, all the newspapers carried the following report:

The Hooliganism of Mr Čaboun

At No. 27 Carmelite Street there lives a former Princely Librarian by
the name of František Čaboun, whose favourite pastime is sprinkling
passing citizens from his window. Yesterday, he went so far as to come
out into the street and attempt to pour water over Councillor Dr
Wollner of the Vice-Regent's Office, whom he had already sprinkled
once before, and when a policeman appeared on the scene, he sprinkled
him and was therefore taken to the police-station, where he was
interviewed and then allowed to go.

From that day forth Mr Čaboun became a complete recluse, and one
fine day he began to throw fuchsias down onto the street.

In the Institution, he works in the garden. Watering the flowerbeds.

1913

Šejba the Burglar Goes on a Job

Šejba the burglar had got himself shut in for the night at Number Fifteen. He was an attic-specialist and for tonight, he had decided to practise his art in this well-off part of town. Up to now, he had been working in a poor area and this had brought him in a grand total of two aprons, three petticoats and a moth-eaten headscarf. In court, this little lot would have got him about six months, whereas the Jew he had sold them to had given him just one crown for the whole bundle.

Šejba was standing in the cellar-area, leaning against the door and listening as the concierge turned down the light, locked the front door and went on her way. By all the signs, she was young, for she was singing softly to herself as she walked from the door to her lodging.

Šejba took this for a good omen. And then, he had met a hay-cart that afternoon. Another good omen. He had seen a chimney-sweep and blown him a kiss: that was good luck as well. He drew a bottle of cheap rum out of his pocket and took a pull at it. Cheap rum: that was what came of working in the poor part of town. Here, it would be a different story. He had had a look round his new patch in the morning and found that it was carpeted all the way up to the first floor. All the signs were that the people who lived here belonged to the well-to-do classes and would have something worth-while in the attic. Feather-beds, let's say, or clothes. He washed down this happy dream with a good swig of rum and sat down on the step by the cellar-door. He was tired, for he'd had the police after him today, down in the river district. It had all been over a handcart with no owner's nameplate on it. He'd hardly gone a few steps when he'd had to take to his heels, minus the cart. He'd got away, thanks be to God, but he felt as if every bone in his body was broken. There was no justice in this world. In the country, you got chivvied by the gendarmes and in town, by the police. Šejba had another swig and heaved a sigh.

There in the house, silence and darkness reigned. Down here by the cellar it was neither warm nor cold, but when Šejba heard his sigh echoing through the quiet of the night, right up to the third floor somewhere, a chill went through him and the thought of what would happen if he got caught crossed his mind. If only they would at least wait till winter before they caught him. He'd spent a few winters in jail in his time. There were some houses of correction now where they'd installed central heating. You were nice and warm, you could eat your fill; the only thing you couldn't get was spirits. You could always rustle up a smoke from somewhere.

Inside the cellar, a cat miaowed. It was on the tip of Šejba's tongue to say 'Puss, puss!' but then he thought better of it. Why take needless risks? It was certain that not everyone in the house would be asleep yet; the concierge might hear him and then the game would be up. He might even get knocked about.

He could hear the cat walking about and miaowing behind the door. It seemed to have got onto the coal: pieces were rolling down from the pile with a noise like thunder. Blast that cat! It was kicking up a racket and what was more, the people on the street would think there was a thief in the cellar.

The idea that anyone might think he had tried to break into a cellar was repugnant to Šejba. Anyone could rob a cellar; an attic now, that was a different story!

He made an angry movement and the skeleton keys in his pocket rattled. This frightened the cat behind the door, which took flight and ran into some heavy object. The bang this made as it fell resounded through the house. He crouched down and listened. The noise rumbled round the house and gradually died away. Not a single voice was raised in response.

He steadied his nerves and took a drink from the bottle. If he had the bad luck to get caught, at least he could make sure the bottle was empty. They wouldn't let him finish it. Somewhere in the house, a bell rang.

'They're ringing for the concierge,' thought Šejba and crouched down again, as if wishing to avoid seeing anything of what was going on around him.

A light shone out of the concierge's lodging and the flip-flop of slippers and the rustle of skirts made themselves heard. The concierge was going to open the door. Šejba hardly dared breathe, in case he should chance to draw attention to himself.

The beam of light broke against the banisters and fell down to the floor opposite Šejba.

'I heard a rumpus in the cellar,' said somebody's voice in the passage, 'so I thought we might have burglars.'

'That's the cats, Mr Councillor Sir,' answered the concierge. 'Every day they make a racket in the cellar. And what they don't get up to in the attic! They trample about up there like devils dancing at a wedding.'

Šejba felt a weight fall from his shoulders. He heard the concierge go back to her lodging and a key rattling in a door up on the second floor. He took advantage of the bustle created by the resident who had got up to have a stretch and a drink of rum.

The light went out and total darkness reigned. Šejba worked out how he would do the job. When it was late he'd sneak up to the attic, open it up, collect anything that was worth having, wait there and early in the morning, immediately the house door was opened, he'd dash out. There weren't many police patrols on the streets at that time of day. And then nature would take its course. With the money he got for the loot, he'd pay his board and lodging, which was already a month overdue. They were poor people and they knew a thing or two about him that could get him into trouble. If it were winter, he wouldn't mind if they turned him in but just now, he wanted to stay outside. It's a peculiar trait of human nature that a man doesn't like to be locked up when the world around him is fresh and green.

Šejba had fallen into what you might say was a mellow mood and when he heard the cat miaowing again in the cellar, he couldn't resist the temptation to give a gentle call of 'Puss, puss!' through the keyhole. The cat ran over to the door and miaowed once more.

Šejba heard it scratching and then it seemed to sit down by the door and purred. Clearly, it was bored, all on its own in the cellar, and was glad that now it had some company, even if they were separated by an impenetrable barrier.

'Why don't I drink her health?' thought Šejba and put this agreeable idea into practice.

Suddenly, he felt safer and stretched his legs, which caused a slight noise. To be on the safe side, he took off his boots.

He managed this without any commotion. Inspired by this success, he swigged some more rum. He stroked the bottle lovingly. It had been his companion on so many jobs. And when he had it filled with rum out of the proceeds, he felt he was giving it its share in his success.

It was his sole companion, the only one he had to talk to during those endlessly tedious hours of waiting in other people's houses, when a man never knows what the next moment may bring.

He held the bottle to his lips and noticed by the gurgling sound that it was now down to only a quarter full. When he couldn't squeeze out a single drop more, he'd go upstairs, and tomorrow he'd fill it up again and say: 'Good girl! You did a great job!'

The rum filled Šejba with a pleasant warmth and carried him up in thought to the attic. It was a well-to-do house; it'd be a well-to-do attic. He recalled the attics in the poor part of town and spat against the door. Two aprons, three petticoats and a moth-eaten headscarf! God, what a drag! Things were going from bad to worse. If they put the price of brandy up again, a bloke might just as well go and hang himself.

He took another swig and his good mood returned. There might be feather-beds up there. You could still get a good price for feathers today. There were just two things it wasn't a total waste of a craftsman's skill to pinch: telegraph wire and feather-beds. You didn't have to half-inch an enormous amount: a little would still get you a jury-trial. How many aprons, petticoats and moth-eaten scarves would it take to do that? A jury was better than a judge sitting alone. He'd been up before a judge any number of times. You always got more prestige out of going before a jury. 'There's a lad,' his colleagues would say, 'he's up for jury-trial!'

'I'll drink the jury's health,' thought Šejba and finished off the contents of the bottle. He'd rest a little longer and then go up the stairs. Nice and slowly, nice and quietly; he dared not make a noise. Holding his boots safely in his hand and barefoot. Why was he feeling angry with himself? Quietly does it. Just hang on a little bit longer and give it a bit more thought. Why not say the Lord's Prayer? That was it: he'd pray first, and then he'd go.

Šejba crept up to the first floor. He held his boots in his hand and paused on every step. You can't be too careful. There he was on the first floor. He groped for the banisters and his hand touched a door. Ah yes, the banisters were on the left. He felt for them and his groping hand again found a door. A bell rang. No doubt about it, he'd pressed the button. His feet turned to lead and he couldn't move a step. And then the door opened and a hand grabbed him by the collar and dragged him into the flat. Into a darkness full of terrors.

Šejba heard a fearsome female voice: 'Breathe on me!'

Šejba breathed, while the terrible hand continued to hold him by the collar.

'So you've descended to drinking rum?' he heard the frightening voice say, in a cutting tone.

'Yes,' answered Šejba, 'I couldn't afford anything else.'

'I see; the great Mr Dorn, Presiding Judge of Court Number One, has to drink his way through all he's got and come down to rum in the end!'

The hand of this terrible woman stroked his face.

'Ah,' thought Šejba, 'she's taken me for Judge Dorn. He tried me not so long ago.'

'Please be so kind as to turn on the light,' Šejba begged.

'So I've got to turn the light on so that the maid can see the state of the Presiding Judge when he comes home!' the woman shouted. 'A fine thing! And you talk to me, your own wife, who couldn't sleep and has been waiting up for you since twelve o'clock, as if I were a stranger! What's that you've got in your hand?'

'My boots, Madam,' Šejba blurted out. The terrible hand ran across his face again.

'He calls me "Madam"; he thinks I'm crazy and he's had his long whiskers shaved off, the miserable wastrel!'

Šejba felt the hand under his nose.

'Ugh! He's clean-shaven, like a common criminal. I swear to God, I'll beat him to a pulp! So that was why he wanted me to turn the light on. The wastrel, he thought I'd be frightened and fall down in a faint and he could go to his room and lock the door.

'Look at him, a Presiding Judge and he looks like a convicted criminal. What's that you've got on your head?'

'A cap.'

'Great God almighty, he gets himself so thoroughly plastered that he leaves his top hat lying about somewhere and buys himself a cap. Or maybe you stole it from someone?'

'Yes, I did steal it,' said Šejba in a penitent tone.

He got another box on the ear and the woman shouted, as she pushed Šejba out through the door: 'You can stay out in the corridor till morning. Let the whole world see what a good-for-nothing layabout Mr Presiding Judge Dorn is!'

She shoved him so hard that he fell over and banged his nose, and locked the door behind him.

'Thank God for that,' thought Šejba as he climbed the stairs. 'It turned out all right in the end.' The only thing was, she'd held onto his boots. His bare feet seemed to him to be shedding a little light on his path, somehow.

He crept up to the second floor. God be praised, he was already passing the door of the first flat without any noise . . . and then all of a sudden, a hand grabbed his collar and dragged him inside.

Šejba found himself surrounded by a darkness even more terrifying than that on the first floor and then, for no reason, he got a slap on the head and a female voice rang out in his ears: 'Kiss my hand!' He kissed the hand and the voice asked: 'Where are your shoes?' Šejba said nothing. He felt the warm hand that he had just kissed running across his bare feet.

He felt himself struck in the back, so hard that he saw stars and heard the words: 'I see, Doctor Peláš, the Examining Magistrate, is not ashamed to come home to his wife drunk and barefoot. What have you done with your stockings, you jailbird?'

Šejba was silent. He was thinking: Examining Magistrate Dr Peláš had been in charge of his last interrogation.

'What have you done with your socks, you jailbird?' the question rang out again.

'I never had any on,' he replied.

'Aha, you're disguising your voice, you villain and you don't know what you're saying.' Šejba felt himself being shaken and his skeleton-keys fell out of his pocket.

'What's that?'

'The keys to the attic,' Šejba replied despondently.

Hardly had he uttered these words than he was thrown out into the corridor. The skeleton-keys came flying out after him followed by the words: 'You're blind drunk, you filthy pig!'

He was about to pick up his keys when someone gripped his arm, gave him a shove and cried: 'No, that really is too much! He gets the whole house up, drinks himself silly and tries to get in through the first door he comes to. What would Mrs Peláš think of that?' And a woman's hand dragged him across to the door opposite, through the hall and into an inside room, where he was dumped onto the sofa. He heard the key turn in the door of an adjoining room and a voice called out: 'It's a good job the Manager can't see you now. A fine cashier he'd think he's got! You can sleep on the divan tonight.'

A quarter of an hour later, Šejba the burglar opened the door and fled from that ill-starred building as if the Devil was after him. And to this day, he doesn't know whether he just imagined it all, or whether it really happened.

He doesn't read the newspapers either, so he hasn't found out in which house it was that his boots, his skeleton-keys and his empty rum-bottle were found.

1913

The Baron's Bloodhound

Pinned to a yellowing door opposite the attic, up on the fourth floor in a god-forsaken back-street, there was a visiting-card which read:

BARON DEKKER OF PŘEHOŘOV

Serving-girls going up to the attic to hang up the washing would often stop outside that door and eavesdrop on the conversation issuing from that superior residence:

'You were saying, Count?'

'Thank you, Baron,' the selfsame voice would reply and then go on: 'I observe that His Excellency is in good spirits. Without doubt, by dear Prince, you were lucky at cards yesterday. What do you say to that, Count?'

'Unless the luck has something to do with that pretty Countess, dear Baron,' said the same voice, 'I'd put my shirt on it. What do you say to a ride today?'

'The horses are ready, gentlemen. *Allons*, then! Where have the hounds got to? *Auf*, Zebor!'

Then the servants would make haste to open the attic door, for a key would rattle in the lock and out of the door would emerge Baron Dekker and behind him, his bloodhound Zebor, he of the sorrowful countenance. The Baron wore a shabby, carefully preserved coat; the bloodhound, it seemed, had on a second-hand skin.

If he had been a horse, he would have looked like Don Quixote's Rocinante.

As it was, there was nothing for it but to trail along after the Baron through this Vale of Tears, one side of him drooping with despondency, the other flaunting the airs and graces of a dog raised in high society.

He had learned this trick from his master.

Outside the house, the Baron was a totally different person. He let everyone feel the full weight of his baronhood. But at home in the evening, back in his lodgings, the old man gave a terrible groan, sat down at his desk and began to write begging-letters to noblemen of all kinds of title and description.

The Baron's bloodhound sat beside him meanwhile, lifting an ear now and again and then turning, with an aristocratic gesture, to look for fleas.

Those confounded fleas! In one of those confidential moments when professional men air their differences, Zebor had said to a dachshund belonging to a huckster down on the street: ''pon my word, those fleas have cost me a good ten years of my life.'

Hearing the scratching of the pen, Zebor stopped rootling about with his nose in the fur on his thigh, twitched one ear and gazed at the Baron with the rheumy eyes of a man who has a cold.

In the begging-letter he was writing to a Count he knew, who was a Captain in the army, the old man was in the process of constructing an enormous fib. He had worked his way so thoroughly into the fiction that he had lost 80,000 crowns and had given his word of honour that he would pay his debt within the week, that he laid down his pen and walked rapidly up and down, declaiming in a loud voice: 'Yes, my dear Count, I must redeem my word of honour; that's the sort of thing, I trust, that doesn't need even to be discussed among gentlemen.'

His bloodhound walked snorting behind him like a shadow and when the Baron sat down once more to continue his begging-letter, he sat down beside him once again and fished a mean and modest titbit out of his fur. When they had finally sent the letter off, the two of them went to bed. Zebor climbed up to his master's feet and through the cold, dingily furnished chamber, the quavering voice of the Baron resounded: 'Zebor, Zebor, where have we got to?'

This was one of those times of deep intimacy, when everything comes to the surface. The hound had his say too: don't imagine that he was a silent partner. When he had had a good grunt, he gave his opinion on the whole matter: 'Well, My Lord, we shouldn't have thrown our money about so wildly.'

'You know, Zebor, just between you and me, we were a pair of numbskulls. What on earth made us take it into our heads to keep so many dancers all at once?'

'Pardon me, My Lord,' growled the bloodhound in reply, 'I didn't keep any dancers, not a single one. And you, My Lord, you were a bit of a card-fiend as well. Was it me, My Lord, that played *trente-quarante*? All I did was chase the hares. Do you remember, My Lord, the time I bit the gamekeeper?'

'Zebor, Zebor,' sighed the Baron in his skimpy feather-bed, 'can you remember the way I used to put down the oysters? Just a nice sprinkling of lemon . . . It makes me cry to think about it . . . and th-then, th-th-then some nice wine on top . . . dammit, Zebor, I'm going to blub!'

'You and me both, My Lord,' growled Zebor and they both had a whine into the feather-bed.

The last thing the old Baron said before he went to sleep was: 'Suppose we won the lottery, Zebor?'

Zebor, who was just nodding off, stirred himself and thought: 'At your service, My Lord.' Then he lay down again and slept on.

They lay like that for two days without eating, until the postman came – with twenty crowns from the Captain.

Then they both got dressed. That is, Zebor licked himself into shape as far as he could reach and the Baron climbed into those faded garments of his, and they stepped ceremoniously out onto the street.

The twenty crowns had warmed the blood in their veins. Zebor knew they were going round the corner and then down the passage-way and on to the other end of town, to a certain shop which had a sign outside bearing a horse's head and the inscription: 'Horsemeat Butcher'.

They marched grandly along, each preoccupied with a vision of smoked horsemeat. And plenty of it.

There was no question, for Zebor, of dallying with other dogs today. One simply didn't have any time to spare for riff-raff of that sort. Today, one was a gentleman. One was going to the shop with the sign of the horse's head.

In the shop, the Baron always manifested certain scruples and would say that he would like three kilograms for a poor widow of his acquaintance who had a large number of children. He would have bought them beef, but would rather spend what he saved on meat to buy stockings for the widow and her children.

And while the Baron was entangling himself in one lie after another, his bloodhound was saying to the butcher's dog: 'We had young sucking-pig yesterday. I ate half a goose, myself.'

And he walked airily away with his master, who was carrying three kilograms of horse-meat. And that night, on a full stomach, they both dreamed they were at the races.

1913

The Purple Thunderbolt

In the year 1596 the purple thunderbolt turned up at the Council of Cardinals in Rome. That was the Council which declared that blasphemers should be struck down by lightning.

This being a matter falling within his professional competence, the purple thunderbolt appeared at the Council, as I have said, out of the blue.

When he got back upstairs afterwards, a complaint was laid against him that he had intruded somewhat too vigorously among the worthy Cardinals and that two of them were bound for the graveyard in consequence. He said that as a matter of fact, he would like to drop in at that funeral; he was sure it would be a really swell affair. It took Saint Peter a long time to explain to him that it would not look very nice if some fresh catastrophe were to occur at the funeral. If it were some secret heretic they were burying, then of course it would be his duty to come crashing down on it.

So the purple thunderbolt sat looking down from Heaven and feeling pleased with himself.

He looked down with contempt at the little thunderbolts playing and frisking about beneath him. Little whippersnappers, they hadn't attended the Council of Cardinals in Rome!

Then he was called before the Lord and came back with his tail between his legs. He had been confined to quarters for a period of six weeks for having blasted those Cardinals at the Council of Rome. And this in the summer-storm season!

In vain he pleaded that the Council had declared that blasphemers should be struck down by lightning and that this concerned him professionally.

When the Archangel Gabriel got round to talking to the purple thunderbolt, he said: 'It's just your rotten luck. You see, you killed that very fat one, the one who made a particularly deep impression on the faithful. You made a right cock-up.'

From that time forth, the purple thunderbolt was very much on his guard against further cock-ups. One day, a certain saint whom he knew by sight only, not by name, came to his cloud, stretched out beside him and started to chat. He launched into an account of the way they had boiled him in oil and of the smell it had made.

This got on the purple thunderbolt's nerves and he said: 'Forgive me, but I've had this up to here. This morning, I must have bumped into at least five martyrs and every one of them described what he'd had done to him before he got here. We've all had a basinful of that stuff. It was all very nice and all very new to start with, but fifteen hundred years of it without any let-up: that's hardly the joys of Heaven!'

'But look here,' said the martyr, 'who else am I supposed to tell about it? I haven't told anyone else yet, because I couldn't remember what kind of oil it was, but today I remembered it was hemp-oil.'

'Oh, for God's sake leave me in peace,' snapped the purple thunderbolt angrily, 'it's enough to try the patience of a saint!'

'But it's really very interesting,' said the martyr. 'Which leg do you reckon got cooked first in that oil, the right one, or the left?'

The purple thunderbolt could stand no more of this nattering and took off down to earth to get away from it.

He travelled in a straight line and when he arrived over the roof of some church or other, was unable to stop himself. He went through the roof and struck the pulpit. Wishing to apologise to the preacher, he hung around for a while, but seeing that the latter was on fire, took fright, fled by way of a certain lady into the earth, and slipped inconspicuously away.

On the flight back to Heaven, he was on the verge of tears. 'Oh dear God,' he said to himself, 'here's another fine mess I've got myself into. I was in too much of a hurry; someone down there might just have had the idea of proclaiming that they had sent a fiery chariot down for him from Heaven, like they did that time it happened to that fellow Elijah. That was a real disaster: it was a relief when they did such a good job of hushing it up down on earth. This time though,' he sighed, 'the preacher will turn up in Heaven and there'll be a complaint made straight away about what I've done to him. Another black mark. Perhaps he'll be up there before I am.'

But the purple thunderbolt's fears were not realised. The following communication was received from the Infernal Information Service: 'A certain Jesuit preacher has just arrived here. It has not yet proved possible to interview him, as he is in a state of shock.'

'Hullo!' said Saint Peter when he heard this news. 'That's another subscriber we've lost.'

Such was the joy of the purple thunderbolt that it had turned out so nicely that he sat for a whole day with a smile on his face, listening to some old fogey going on with relish about the time he had had his intestines drawn out. He made a meal of it, of course; three hundred and seventy-two metres was the figure he quoted.

Then a report came in from Hell to the effect that the preacher had been interviewed and was claiming that it was the purple thunderbolt that had done this thing to him.

But against his expectations, he got a commendation. 'He wasn't really worth the effort, the ruffian,' they told him at the hearing, 'but you did well. You've undermined confidence in the priesthood, it's true, but at any rate, you can look forward to a job with more satisfaction in future. We are appointing you to the permanent job of blasting blasphemers.'

'As laid down by the Council of Rome,' added the purple thunderbolt and set off on reconnaissance.

He found himself a nice dark cloud with a good view of the world below and excellent acoustics. He could hear every word spoken down there.

'Aha!' thought the purple thunderbolt after he had listened for a while. 'This looks like a job for me.' And he continued to observe developments.

In a cottage down below, a red-headed fellow was lying in bed and sitting beside him was a man who, by the look of him, was either a parish priest or a chaplain.

'Come now, Macoun, it's time you mended your ways. You can see that God has punished you: you can't move a muscle.'

'I've got it in the small of me back and I can't stand on me feet neither!'

'And yet you go on using bad language.'

'Well I ask you, sod the bloody thing; what sort of a life do you call this? Damn and blast it to Hell!'

The purple thunderbolt could contain himself no longer and launched himself downwards at the red-headed fellow.

'Wham!' He hit the cottage and the cottage fell down, but now he was sliding downwards along some slippery part of the bed, trying to stop himself and grabbing at His Reverence's hand. The latter went tumbling over and the purple thunderbolt panicked, fled into the pigsty and on up into the sky, where he paused and looked down to see what he had done. They were carrying His Reverence out and tolling the funeral bell and Macoun was walking about in his parlour, saying: 'Well damn me if it hasn't gone!'

He told this to an old saint with many years of experience, who said to him: 'Don't you know that a man in a feather-bed can curse and blind as much as he likes? And don't you know that a feather-bed is a bad conductor while a priest is a good one?'

'But on top of everything, Macoun can walk!'

'Well, what do you expect,' said the saintly old-stager in a sour tone of voice, 'when you've just given him electric shock therapy.'

The purple thunderbolt burst into tears.

1913

The Battle for Souls

I

Father Michalejc was a saint on a stipend of three thousand crowns a year, to which was added a whole string of other emoluments from the eight communities attached to his parish of Svobodné Dvory. These communities were dispersed among the ancient forests in the mountains round about and the people who lived there were for the most part lumbermen who would come down to the church in Svobodné Dvory once every three months. And then they would say a great many prayers, enough to last them for the next three months, make confession, receive the Body of the Lord with an ecstasy and awe that were beyond description and perform their penances with the utmost seriousness. Then they would go over to the Mid-Day, the inn behind the presbytery, and bit by bit, the inhibitions that held their tongues in check would fall away. Delivered from their sins and exalted by the mystery of that sacramental transubstantiation, they would become more boisterous than the inhabitants of Svobodné Dvory could bear.

And the tensions in the Mid-Day would develop into brawls between the men of the valley and those of the eight mountain villages, who had just had three months' worth of sins taken away. Having occasioned damage both to the Mid-Day Inn and to the heads of the men of Svobodné Dvory, the loggers from the mountains would retire, their shoulders laden with new sins and their backs with bruises, to their mountain forests and peace would descend for another three months.

And then, three months later, those tall, angular figures would come striding down the mountainside into the valley, their faces full of contrition, and the church would be filled with the booming voices of these quarterly sinners, which could be heard over on the village green. And when they said the Lord's Prayer, it sounded from a distance like two people shouting across from one mountain-slope to another: 'Václav, what are you up to?' And the cries of the penitents sounded with a mighty roar when Father Michalejc in his wooden pulpit thundered out one of the eight sermons with which he would chastise the inhabitants of all nine villages.

But he was wasting his breath. It is true that tears of emotion would trickle down many a weatherbeaten cheek but once they had done their penance, the burly men of the mountains would just go off to the pub for a punch-up.

During these bouts of violence, Father Michalejc would shut himself in his room, from which he had a good view of the Mid-Day Inn, and from behind the curtain observe his faithful flock, and as and when he saw one of the lumbermen fighting outside the inn, would jot down the details in his notebook in an entirely businesslike spirit: 'Bočan, forty Our Fathers, Kryšpín, twenty Our Fathers and look at Antonín Dlouhý there, jumping on the Mayor! That's fifty Our Fathers for you, my lad, and you don't get off a single Amen! Černouch: well, if you don't want a beating, don't get into a fight. I'll give you just fifteen Hail Marys.'

So it went on and Father Michalejc would conscientiously enter the names of the loggers in his book and when penance-time came round again, each of the men from the mountains would receive a slip of paper on which his appointed quota and type of prayer had been copied from the notebook.

And it would all go like clockwork and in proper order as one after another they knelt on the stool in the old, worm-eaten confessional and let rip in emotional tones: 'I confess to Almighty God and to You, Venerable Father, that after Holy Communion, I got into a fight at the Mid-Day Inn.' That was the principal sin. It would be followed by another series, consisting always of the identical transgressions: taking the name of the Lord in vain, cursing and swearing with the first words that came into their heads, 'pinching a log or two from the boss' and 'setting a snare when I shouldn've.'

For fifteen years, four times a year, it was always the same and only once in all that time did it occur that Bočan omitted the 'snare when I shouldn've' from his confession. With a delicate reproach in his voice, Father Michalejc turned to the penitent: 'And what about the odd snare, eh, Bočan?'

'You're bark'n' up the wrong tree there, Your Reverence,' said Bočan. 'Could'n' do no snarin' this time: some bugger run off with me wires and I could'n' get down to town for a new lot. Bunch of thieves they are up our way, Your Reverence.'

That, though, was the one and only time when one of them at least had a sin missing from the usual list but in his next confession, Bočan no longer deviated from his normal declaration and Father Michalejc derived a sort of comfort from hearing once more the sorrowful pronouncement: 'An' I set a snare when I shouldn've.'

I say that Father Michalejc was comforted by this, for he was fond of those burly mountain-folk and he knew from experience that if the snare did not make its scheduled appearance, there was something bodily and spiritually amiss with the man in question and he hadn't got long to go. Fifteen years of experience as a spiritual shepherd teaches you things like that. First the snares stopped coming, then there would be no mention of logs and the sinner would not drop in at the Mid-Day after completing his devotions, but climb laboriously back up to his home in the wooded mountains. And when his wife came running down to the priest's house to complain that her husband hadn't let out a 'Goddam' or 'Bloody Hell' for a whole day, then priest and sexton set out for the mountains straight away, hoping to be able to administer extreme unction while the poor devil was still alive.

His fifteen years' experience had taught Father Michalejc that he was not going to make his mountain-dwelling parishioners from the eight attached communities any better, not by the finest preaching, nor by the most passionate exhortation, bitterly as they might weep; they themselves acknowledged that the endeavour was pointless.

At first, he had tried to explain to them the need for a resolution to live in holiness and righteousness for the rest of their days, but at the end of his careful exposition of the doctrine, Valoušek from Černkov had said to him: 'Your Reverence, we'll leave all this holiness and righteousness stuff to the young folk. Anyway, if things go on the way they have been, the game will've died off and a man won't be able to trap anything in a month of Sundays.'

And ten years ago, Chudomel had taken him by the hand and said, frank as could be: 'Your Reverence, we just aren't goin' to get any better. Whatever you do, them devils is going to be turning us round over the fire on their pitchforks. 'twill be as God wills.' And so Father Michalejc became accustomed to the way things were. He had a piece of woodland up there in the mountains beyond Černkov in Wolf Valley and one day Pavlíček said to him in the quarterly confessional: 'There was a log or two belonging to the boss, Your Reverence and then I went into that wood, you know, Your Reverence, the one that sort of belongs to you, and I kind of took a log . . . 'twas a very hard winter this year. So I cut down four spruces from Your Reverence's wood and with every one that I cut down, I said an Our Father for you. And all of a sudden I felt as if a weight had fallen off me and there was such a lightness in my heart that I cut down another three.' Chudomel got ten Our Fathers for the landlord's wood and thirty for the priest's, both as a penance and as a warning that a priest was God's representative on earth and if you rob your priest, it's the same as if you were to cut down the trees of the Lord God Himself.

After these experiences, Father Michalejc tried to persuade his patron to be so kind as to exchange his woodland in the mountains for something in the vicinity of Svobodné Dvory but when these attempts failed, got used to the fact that they were stealing from him in the full knowledge that it was the same as cutting down the trees of the Lord God Himself.

Surrounded by sinners like these, Father Michalejc's resolve to strive for the moral betterment of such people ebbed with the passage of the years, for whenever he met one of them his exhortations were received with a sigh of hopelessness: 'Well now, Father, 'tes a waste of your time talkin' t' us, I b'lieve. We ain't no good, none of us.'

And this was said with such heartfelt sincerity that after fifteen years of battling against this 'moral insanity' (in the English jargon) on the part of his mountain-dwelling parishioners, Father Michalejc laid aside his notebook and stopped registering the quotas of penitential Our Fathers for each individual. At the quarterly sessions, he would reel off his stereotyped sermons on sin and the consequences of sin completely mechanically. His style lost the colour of younger days and he was only stirred to passion when Povondra, for example, started to haggle over his Our Fathers. That Povondra was as hard a bargainer as any Jewish trader and would make Father Michalejc an offer of half the required amount: 'No more than fifteen Our Fathers, Your Reverence. I'd be hard put to it to get any real warmth into the sixteenth and by the time it came to number thirty, I'd be loading another mortal sin onto my soul. I've tried, Reverence, really I have, but from fifteen to thirty, I was just swallowing them down and I was through them in two shakes of a duck's tail.'

Even to this Father Michalejc became inured, and he even gave up arguing against Bočan's theory that by the time you'd done three Our Fathers, God had already forgiven you because all good things came in threes, and so the others were just so much wasted effort.

Wearied by this battle for the welfare of the souls of his mountain flock, Father Michalejc omitted, one day, to ask for details when

Mareš from Kořenkov sorrowfully replied, when asked what he had to confess: 'Same as last time, Your Reverence.' Stoically, he gave absolution without adding any admonitions and would even have forgotten to impose a penance if Mareš himself hadn't reminded him: 'Same Our Fathers as usual, Your Reverence?'

Sometimes he felt a renewal of the energy he had once had, when he arrived in Svobodné Dvory years before and when, a quarterly influx of penitents due, he would open one of the volumes of his *Preachers' Yearbook* to dig out some material for a sermon capable of transforming the soul of a sinner, but then he would look at the hard outlines of the mountains, as solid as the principles of his mountain-dwelling parishioners, shut the book and go off to the Mid-Day Inn for a game of tarock.

And finally, he found himself in retreat across the whole front. And as they noticed how resigned he had become, they gradually began to leave sins out. Gradually, the logs disappeared, then the 'snare when I shouldn've', the cursing and swearing and the fighting at the Mid-Day Inn, and one fine day it came to pass that Zamečníček from Horní Bourov, after reeling off the formula: 'I confess to Almighty God and to you, worthy Father,' added in a tone of exaltation: 'that I am as pure as a lily, Your Reverence!'

On that very same day, the disconsolate Father Michalejc sent a request in to the Consistory for a chaplain with real drive.

II

The dynamic chaplain was a man by the name of Müller. He was as thin as one of those ascetics who could hold out to the glory of God, standing on a pillar, for a whole week without eating. It was impossible to guess from his pale face how old he was, but this much was clear: in amongst those severe, dessicated features, the manly joys of youth had vanished without trace. Not that his eyes were animated by any spark of heavenly inspiration. Even in his moments of greatest excitement, those eyes resembled the grey, watery soup they serve up in a seminary on fast-days. As for his speech, he enunciated each individual syllable as precisely as if he were speaking the Aramaic of Biblical times.

The dynamic chaplain had a stammer. The Consistory's gift to Svobodné Dvory was a severe shock to Father Michalejc and the latter's sister, who acted as housekeeper for him, walked about the house like a ghost for the whole of the first day. After the formalities of arrival, the dynamic chaplain expounded to them in a speech which, as a result of his habit of giving Aramaic impressions, took more than two hours to deliver, how he had been a missionary in Port Said for two years and had 'c-c-converted a m-m-m-mullah.' Then he had returned to Moravia, where he had been a chaplain in Tišnov, 'g-got to g-g-grips with g-g-g-gambling' and 't-t-totally eradicated it.' Now, he was here.

Over supper Father Michalejc gave him an account, punctuated with copious sighs, of his fifteen-year experience of the area and the dynamic chaplain, nibbling at a piece of bread, pushed away the plate full of smoked meat and said: 'I don't approve of m-m-meat-eating and I intend to r-root it out. I shall give them a g-g-good t-t-talking-to. I-I-I shall enlighten them with the H-H-H-Holy S-Spirit!' Then, turning his eyes up to the ceiling and fixing them on the hook from which the lamp hung, he cried out prophetically: 'I shall c-c-convert them!'

Father Michalejc set out for a game of tarock and the dynamic chaplain went off to his chapel to pray from his breviary.

God knows how it came about, but the very next day, when the dynamic chaplain was on his way to the woods carrying some theological tome or other, he heard a child's voice behind a bush say: 'C-Convertamullah!' Then a shadowy childish figure flitted through the trees and vanished with a cry of 'Hoo!' into the graveyard.

'Sh-shocking m-m-manners!' said the dynamic chaplain to himself and sitting down at the edge of the forest, began to make a few notes: 'When I last made confession, was I properly prepared and in the right frame of mind? Am I certain that I did not omit any sins? Have I completed my penance? Can I remember the admonitions and warnings I received? Have I not sinned since then?'

The dynamic chaplain gazed at the mountains and shook his fist in that direction with a cry of: 'I'll sh-sh-show them!'

Within a week, it was known through the mountains that the 'fine young gen'lman' had 'c'nverted a mullah'. Bočan, who was working on a fir-tree with Fanfulík the other side of Baba, said to his mate: ''e's got the gift of the gab all right! Last Christmas, when he was still in Moravia, he struck up: "Jesus Christ is born", but 'e won' get round to the "Rejoice" bit till our service 'ere, this Christmas coming.'

'They say 'e wants t' lead us back to the path of righteousness', said Fanfulík, and spat in contempt.

''e can try till 'e's blue in the face,' said Bočan calmly. ''tes all wasted on us.'

And then Chudomel, chatting with Valoušek from Černkov, remarked: 'Well, if our old gent couldn't take away our sins, old "Convertamullah" certainly won't.'

And through the mountains, the unshakeable conviction established itself that the sudden appearance of the chaplain in Svobodné Dvory was an infringement of their rights. This brought about an increase in the sylvan crime-rate.

When news of this reached the ears of the dynamic chaplain, he cried out in a voice fired with conviction: 'I'll c-c-convert them!' and burrowed deeper into his theological books.

But the penitents from the mountains did not give in so easily. Before confession, they listened to his ardent, persuasive, hour-long general exhortation to the effect that 'Th-thousands of p-p-people had already been l-lost' and that 'the same f-f-fate' awaited them, and were deeply moved. Yes, they said, with a sad shake of the head, it was all true and then in they came to confession with innocent looks on their faces and just like Zamečník from Horní Bourov, declared themselves free from sin.

With many a stutter, the chaplain refused to give them absolution and threatened them with eternal punishment. The words rang out from the confessional: 'What about those l-logs then? the s-snares? Th-think of Eternity', followed immediately by the innocent, emphatic reply: 'Dedn' set no snares, Young Reverence, dedn' take no logs!'

There were those among them who were carrying in their pockets a summons to appear before their secular judge in the District Court a few days after this appearance before their spiritual one, but these too denied the snares and logs with the serenity of martyrs, being firmly convinced that in the matter of eternal damnation, there was nothing that anyone could do.

''tes no use,' said the penitents from the mountains, 'even if the Archbishop himself were to come, let alone old "Convertamullah" here.'

III

The dynamic chaplain fought the good fight for the souls of the parishioners from the mountains for a full two years and gave Father Michalejc a great deal of satisfaction in the process. In vain did the chaplain strive to instil some kind of moral responsibility into them. The attitude of the men from the mountains was conveyed to Father Michalejc by Bočan when they met one day up in the hills: 'Y'know, Your Reverence, 'tes hard. We aren' goin' let'n steal our sins away from us. Honesty, that's for the rich folks; ain't no respectable people been born among us up to now.'

'But why won't you repent of your sins, Bočan?'

'We do repent, we do; but 'e's trying to convert us and as Your Reverence d' know, we're a hopeless lot. Now if only he, that's the young gen'lman, would stop going on all the time 'bout damnation. You, Your Reverence, you used't tell us some 'andsome tale 'bout 'ow they devils would melt us down for candle-grease, but you never said nothin' 'bout damnation. Damnation's for rich folks; cauldrons and brimstone's good enough for us poor people. And if only the Young Reverence would at least stop telling us we can't fight no more an' that we've got to stop stealing an' swearing. Believe it or not, 'e wuddn' 'ere five minutes 'fore 'e started telling us not to do things.'

Bočan paused for breath and then went on, speaking with a delicate warmth in his voice and an affectionate glance at Father Michalejc: 'You wuddn' like that, Your Reverence, you was kind to us an' in all them fifteen years, you never once said to us: "Don't do that no more." You just used to talk 'bout the old sins but when it came to those we might do 'tween one confession and another, you never warned us off them, Your Reverence.'

This outpouring had such an effect on Father Michalejc that he had to sit down on an overturned tree-trunk. It had hit him like a bolt from the blue and what was more, it was the melancholy truth. He remembered that in actual fact he had never warned them against future sins in all those fifteen years. He turned his remorseful eyes up to heaven as Bočan went on in an intimate tone: ''tes just the way we're born, you see. 'twas like when you d' do a job of work. We came feeling sorry and said we'd stolen this an' that from the boss, we'd been fightin', we'd damned and blasted and then you, Your Reverence, would say we 'ad to make a sincere resolve to repent and we'd repent and scrape about on our knees and say: "Lord God, forgive us miserable sinners." But you didn' say nothin' 'bout what we was going to do and we recited all them Our Fathers gladly, 'cos they was for the old sins, not the new ones, or the old ones *and* the new ones, like the Young Reverence wants us t'do; because 'e d' say twenty for the old ones and another twenty for the new ones that's still to come. That eddn' fair, Your Reverence. Our boss only pays us for the trees we've cut down, not for those we're going to cut down tomorrow. The Young Reverence now, when 'e goes on like that, 'e d' take our sins away from us in advance and that eddn' proper repentance. And if we've worked them off in advance, then we're bound to be pure when we d' come to confession, but he won't believe us, even though he went an' let us off them beforehand. And so we *has* to say we 'avn' set no snares nor pinched no logs, 'cos we've already done the penance for them in advance.'

And saluting the Father like a good Christian, Bočan took his axe and strode off up the slope and Father Michalejc continued to gaze remorsefully heavenwards and then went sadly off to report Bočan's views to Chaplain Müller. The dynamic chaplain heard him out, nodding his head sadly, and said: 'I too can s-see that they're a b-b-bunch of riff-raff!' And that evening, he wrote and respectfully requested the Consistory to allow him to give up this post and take the missionary trail once more to Asia Minor. 'For the purpose of c-converting m-m-mullahs!'

IV

Two months later, a new chaplain appeared at the presbytery in Svobodné Dvory. A jolly young man and a real treasure as far as Father Michalejc was concerned, for he could play tarock.

After three months, the word had spread across the mountains that here was an angel and one day, Zamečník from Horní Bourov came into the presbytery and kissing the Father's hand respectfully, said in a grateful voice: 'Praised by Christ Jesus, Your Reverence, the new young gen'l'man we've got as chaplain is right up our street. He don't ask us 'bout the old stuff, nor the new stuff; he d' know it's all a waste of time, you see. A angel he is an' 'e d' call us such lovely names at confession that we breaks down and cries like old women.'

With these words, he dragged into the room a sack that he had left outside the door and said to Father Michalejc in a friendly tone: 'I'd be much obliged to you, Your Reverence, if you would give this doe to the new young gen'l'man. Caught 'er in me snare last night, I did; she's a real beauty. An' if you would please tell him that 'tes out of gratitude because he d' do it so lovely when he calls us bloody thieves.'

Before Father Michalejc could recover himself, Zamečník shook the doe out of the sack and vanished like an apparition.

And so there on the carpet, in front of the parish priest, there lay a doe: the final summation of a seventeen-year battle for the souls of the penitents from the mountains.

V

And when, before midday three days later, the Mayor was passing the open windows of the presbytery kitchen, he stopped, sniffed the vapours drifting through the window and cried: 'Well, I'll be damned if that isn't venison I can smell!' And with his head full of agreeable thoughts, he went on past the presbytery, where they were just laying the table for dinner.

1913

The Tourist Guide

in the South German Town of Neuburg

'Four marks and all I eat and drink.' Those were the terms on which Herr Jogelli Klopter advertised his guided tour of the town of Neuburg on the Danube.

That final stipulation gave me an uneasy feeling. For the paunch of Herr Jogelli Klopter was one of abnormal proportions, even when measured by Bavarian standards of corpulence.

And the normal Bavarian scale does not register a weight lower than ninety kilograms.

The tourist will always find that it pays to haggle with his guide. So I haggled quite bluntly. 'You look like a hearty eater to me,' I said. 'Now if you were thinner . . .'

Herr Jogelli took on a mournful look. 'Even thinner!' he sighed. 'Great God Almighty, you ought to have seen my late father. Not to speak of my late grandfather! He'd eat a whole ham, a dish full of dumplings and a bowlful of salad, just for a snack, as you might say.'

'I'll give you three marks extra,' I said. 'Seven marks for the day.'

'*Herrgott!*' answered Herr Jogelli with characteristic Teutonic elegance. 'Then you're a skinflint and you can go round the town on your own. But don't cross my path. Do you think, Mister, that Jogelli Klopter is out to fleece the visitors? He's happy with the odd litre of beer and the odd snack now and again.'

This was the second time I'd heard the word 'snack' fall from his lips and it sent a chill down my spine but then I remembered that a tourist should try to make as few enemies as he can on his travels, especially when they're as well covered as this one was. So we shook hands on it, he got his four marks and stood me a mug of beer downstairs.

This is a custom observed by all Bavarian guides. A little present to cement the friendship and then they get it back out of you twenty times over in the course of the day.

Not a lot of tourists visit Neuburg. It could be that Herr Jogelli Klopter is to blame for this, but not a lot of tourists visit this part of Germany in any case.

The countryside around Neuburg is not particularly attractive. Every small town and every village in this area has very much the same character. And here and there, wherever there was the ruin of an old castle, they have restored it and turned it into a brewery. The Bavarians are a very enterprising people when it comes to that sort of thing. In Genderkingen, for example, Mertingingen, Dürzlenkingen, Bersheimingen, Irgelsheimingen and all the endless other 'ingens' (the names round here are as monotonous as the newspapers). Social life in all these 'ingens' revolves around the feuds between the individual 'ingens' and the violent punch-ups in the pubs of each separate 'ingen'. It's at its worst in the Neuburg area. In this brutal environment, Herr Jogelli Klopter had spent his formative years.

Neuburg itself is a quaint old town, which is something you could say about each and every Bavarian town. If I were writing a travel-book, I would say that it has two gateways, but as it is, I will just point out that I entered the town one evening through one gateway and left it next morning through the other. And for this last circumstance, Herr Jogelli Klopter definitely is to blame.

Neuburg also possesses the walls of a castle, which are maintained in a miserable condition. Some time or other in centuries past, the Swedes smashed those walls to bits and the Neuburgers have left them in precisely that same state ever since. Another factor that could account for this is that they always vote for conservative candidates.

Like any self-respecting Bavarian town, Neuburg has a *Rathaus* in the Old German style. This *Rathaus* has a long flight of steps leading up to it. This was the sum-total of the information imparted to me by Herr Jogelli on this subject. The Danube branches into two arms at this point. To this, too, Herr Jogelli drew my attention. And as we were crossing the bridge, he announced that this bridge was made of wood.

At the entrance to the bridge stands a sentry wearing a *Pickelhaube*. Why he was standing there, Herr Jogelli did not know and I'm pretty certain that the soldier himself hasn't the faintest idea either.

When we got to the other side, Herr Jogelli announced that this was the end of the bridge. Perhaps you imagine that apart from the *Rathaus* and the wooden bridge, he did not draw my attention to anything else? Far from it! Between the *Rathaus* and the end of the bridge there are five breweries and eight inns. Beyond the last inn stands the gateway and it was through that gateway that I left the town, a town that houses the archive of the 'Schwabenland' and surrounding areas, and also Herr Jogelli Klopter, whom I can recommend most warmly to all tourists.

When we had left the inn where I had spent the night and crossed the bridge, my worthy guide said: 'I will now show you the ancient Ship Inn.' The exterior was not very prepossessing. 'We have to go in,' said Herr Jogelli. 'We've got to wait here for a man.' This was said in such a good-humoured tone that I was in no doubt that the tourist guide wanted to have a drink and get back with interest what he had stood me to seal our agreement, and that 'waiting for a man' was just a formula that enabled him to invoke the supplementary clause of that agreement, namely: 'all I eat and drink.'

I ordered beer. Herr Jogelli took a swig and began to speak: 'I'm waiting for a no-good specimen. A *Schweinkerli* he is, a real *Schweinbübli*.' He came out with a selection of names, formed from various combinations based on the word *Schwein*, took another pull and went on: 'I've got a bone to pick with that fellow, Sir, a very big bone indeed. And when he turns up, there'll be some fun and games. He's from Dürzlenkingen and I'm from Bersheimingen. We Bersheimingers are *roh*, *awer gutmütig* but that Dürzlenkingen lot are just *roh*; not a trace of good nature. Rubbish and *Schweinbüblis*, that's all there is in Dürzlenkingen.'

'*Schweinkerli*,' I remarked, just to be saying something.

'That's right, *Schweinkerli*,' said Herr Jogelli. 'And you won't find a bigger *Schweinkerli* than Johannes Bewign.'

He emptied his mug and ordered himself another. 'We,' he said, becoming excited, 'we Bersheimingers have never got on with that riff-raff from Dürzlenkingen. You see, every village round here talks differently, but they're so bad in Dürzlenkingen that they can't understand us Bersheimingers. My father in Bersheimingen was a "pa-a" but that Johannes has always laughed at me and said that he doesn't know what a "pa-a" is. The *Schweinbübli*!'

'Excuse me, Herr Jogelli, what exactly is a "pa-a"?'

'A pa-a is a pa-a, Sir. How can I put it any better in German?'

(To this day, I do not know what a 'pa-a' is, so according to Herr Jogelli I am a *Schweinbübli*).

'Ha! Do you know, that good-for-nothing Johannes came here to Neuburg to make competition for me and he's putting it about that I'm a drunkard. A fine tourist-guide he is, that Johannes Bewign; as soon as he gets his hooks into a tourist, he drinks himself and the tourist-gentleman into a stupor. The pig! So we wait for him. And I'll say to him: "There you are, *Schweinbübli*, you can't put one over on me. I can attract a better class of tourist than you can, you miserable Dürzlenkingen creature." And if we don't find him here, he's sure to be at the Burgsheim brewery and if he isn't there, he'll be somewhere in the inns around the *Rathaus*, or a brewery up by the Castle, and if he hasn't shown his face even up there, we'll look for him in the Last Gate Inn.'

'And suppose he isn't there either, Herr Jogelli?'

The tourist guide pounded the table with his fist. 'Then we'll go after him all the way to Dürzlenkingen!'

A very pleasant chap, this Jogelli Klopter, as you can see.

A pearl beyond price, that tourist-guide of mine! He knew the place down to the minutest detail. He was a mine of information. He held forth at length. When we left the Ship, we went along a narrow street. As we turned the corner, Herr Jogelli stopped in front of an old building. 'They killed a butcher from Weidling here last year,' he said darkly, pointing to the building. 'That's the Burgsheim brewery.'

'And who was it who killed him, Herr Jogelli?'

'People from Dürzlenkingen, Sir. This is where they congregate. Perhaps my rival, Johannes Bewign, will be here. You go first.'

When we were sitting at a table, Herr Jogelli passed an expert eye over a number of gigantic figures who were quarrelling with each other over in a dimly-lit corner.

'He's not among that lot,' he said in a disappointed tone. 'The two on the right live in Regensburgstrasse and those two on the left on the Augsburg road, they'll go on squabbling like that for another hour before they start on each other. Nothing interesting there. A pity there's no-one here from Friedrichsplatz or the Pfalzstrasse. Those boys know a thing or two about fighting. Or somebody from the Lesheim suburb, or Hein.'

He spat. 'This lot,' he said despairingly, 'don't know one end of a knife from the other. We ought to get the Dürzlenkingen mob onto them. They cut that Weidling butcher up a fair treat. They'd never have got me like that. A pity Johannes Bewign isn't here. But we'll find him, Sir, and if he gives us any lip, we'll sort him out.'

As you can see, Herr Jogelli Klopter never gives his foreign tourists short measure as do many tourist guides, who conduct their tours at a gallop, to get them over as soon as possible.

Neuburg, then, is an old-world town. It has many an old-world house and among those pretty houses, with their oriel windows and pantiles, is the one that contains the Big Pipe Inn. This hostelry displays a notice which reads: 'Prompt Payment Appreciated.' It's a dark and gloomy place with an old vaulted ceiling which threatens to collapse onto the customers' heads. With this in mind, it has been propped up with two wooden beams. Some Bersheimingen Samson could bury a whole company of Dürzlenkingers by pulling those beams down. Herr Jogelli was subject to biblical impulses of this kind. 'If there were too many of them for me to handle,' he said with narrowed eyes, 'I know what I'd do. I'd do what Samson did.'

Herr Johannes Bewign was not in the Big Pipe. After waiting for him in vain, we proceeded further on our way.

'We'll go to the Monastery Brewery,' my guide informed me. 'The Monastery Brewery is remarkable for the fact that . . .'

'Here we go,' I thought, 'now for a boring lecture along the lines of: "This building dates from the sixteenth century . . ." and so on.'

'Have you tasted the Neuburg leberwurst yet?' said Herr Jogelli, interrupting my train of thought.

'I had some yesterday, in the inn where I stayed the night.'

'In that case, you haven't had real leberwurst. The Monastery Brewery is remarkable for the fact that the Franciscan fathers here make such good leberwurst that apart from the miraculous image of Saint Heliodorus, which attracts visitors from all over the Schwabenland, the pilgrims come here for the leberwurst from as far away as the Upper Palatinate. There are times in the brewery when two processions get into one another's hair and start a punch-up and do you know what the Franciscan fathers do in a case like that? They take their leberwurst away. That soon stops the brawling.'

[The conversation continues in the Monastery Brewery itself.]

'And why do they fight among themselves, Herr Jogelli?'

'On account of the image of Saint Heliodorus, Sir. Every procession wants to be the first to kiss the image, so that they can be the first to go and eat the leberwurst, because there isn't a tastier snack to be found anywhere.'

Herr Jogelli consumed a two-pound snack of this delicacy. This turned out to be a really lucky hostelry for us. We found out that Herr Jogelli's rival, Johannes, had left half an hour ago with a tourist and had set out for one of the breweries up by the Castle, and that he had been asking after Herr Jogelli.

'That scoundrel!' exclaimed Herr Jogelli with a dramatic flourish. 'So he's got hold of some miserable little tourist after all, has he? There's nothing for it; we've got to follow the two of them up to the Castle. It looks as if they are both afraid of us.'

Herr Jogelli was becoming more and more intimate in his manner.

'You,' he said, 'can take care of the tourist.'

He said this in a determined tone which meant: 'He who is not with me is against me.'

There are five breweries attached to the Castle, snuggled up against it like chicks against a mother-hen. The people of Neuburg placed what they held most dear under the protection of the Castle.

During the Thirty Years' War, a band of Swedes had forced their way up to the Castle and after a bitter battle, captured the first brewery. And there, the victors had got themselves thoroughly plastered. When the Castle garrison saw this, they made a sortie, but they had to pass the second brewery on the way. The garrison could not resist the temptation and driven by the anxiety that if they did not drink the beer that was stored there, the Swedish mercenaries would, they attacked the barrels in the second brewery rather than the Swedes in the first. And they overpowered those barrels. They drank them dry. The Swedes, meanwhile, had recovered and mounted an assault on the second brewery. They found it occupied and moved on to Number Three, where they drank at such length that they got themselves into an even more inebriated state than they had been in Number One. They met with no resistance. Meanwhile, however, the garrison in Number Two had come round and moved out to protect Number Three. But they were too late. All they found were sleeping Swedes and empty barrels. Enraged by the sight of the empty barrels, they slaughtered the Swedes. And that was the Victory of Neuburg, as it is known, which is recorded in the inscription under the device on the Castle gate.

'They deserved their fate,' said Herr Jogelli gravely, standing under the device. 'The Swedes did a lot of damage at that time. According to the history books, there were many more breweries in the Schwabenland before the Thirty Years' War than there are today.'

Today, as I have said, there are only five of them by the Castle. In none of these historically significant sites did Herr Jogelli find his rival guide Johannes, or I my rival tourist.

'The main thing is,' Herr Jogelli instructed me when he emerged, disappointed, from the last one, 'not to let anyone get close to you. You grab your mug and throw it, pick up your chair and throw it, pull a leg off the table and throw that. That's the best way.'

'I don't have much hope,' he said, as we made our way along the passageway to the Castle gateway, 'of finding that ruffian in the Last Gate Inn. Suppose they're playing games with us?'

Never give up hope! We did find them in the Last Gate. The competitor-tourist was looking around him with an apprehensive expression, Herr Johannes with an aggressive one.

We sat down opposite them. The other tourist and Herr Johannes were on intimate terms. They clinked mugs. 'Now then, old son,' I heard Herr Johannes advise the apprehensive tourist in a loud voice, 'you go over to that stranger and clock him one and I'll take care of the rest as far as Jogelli is concerned.'

At that very moment, Herr Jogelli pronounced, in a voice like thunder: 'Everyone from Dürzlenkingen is a *Schweinkerli!*'

'And the Bersheimingers are a load of *Schweinbübli!*' shouted Herr Johannes.

And at one and the same moment, Jogelli's mug and Johannes's mug went flying through the air. After which there was a free-for-all, for there were a number of people there from Lesheim suburb and Hein and they took advantage of this opportunity to indulge in a little mutual head-cracking.

Under cover of the rumpus I slipped away, and outside the door I met the other tourist. 'We'd been looking for you in all the breweries and pubs,' said the other tourist. 'Johannes kept saying that he had some bone or other to pick with Jogelli, who was making competition for him.'

We went through the gate and out of Neuburg.

'A nice place,' said the other tourist with enthusiasm. 'Back in Württemberg, where I come from, it's all too tame.'

There you are, then! Now you know what the Germans are like, and what kind of tourist guides they have in the South German town of Neuburg, on the Danube.

1913

The Coffin-Dealer

Mr Lindiger was one of those people on whom Fortune never smiles. Even when he was on his way to be christened, the woman who was carrying him to church, all neatly wrapped, was within an ace of getting herself picked up, for no reason at all, on the horns of a runaway bullock. On the very day that he got his first pair of trousers, so that even from a distance, his masculinity was plain for all to see, he somehow found himself hanging, by those same trousers, from a nail in the wooden bridge over the stream. And another misfortune followed relatively quickly after that, and then a whole string of accidents.

As for example when he fell from the attic onto his mother's prize gander and killed it.

He himself, it must be said, suffered no injury and he even described with relish how enjoyable it was falling on top of a goose: just like falling on a feather-bed. But his mother took a different view and this was the first occasion on which young Frantík came into contact with the switch which continued from then on to play an active part in his family life.

At the same time, no-one should assume that the young Lindiger brought these disasters on his head out of wilfulness. The catastrophes came upon him of their own accord . . . one misfortune departed, to make way for another. At school one day, he was lying in wait behind the door with a ruler for one of his friends and it was simply a matter of course that it was the Headmaster, who had unexpectedly opened the door at just that moment, whom he whacked on the nose with it.

And later, when he had reached the age when any man worth his salt ought to fall in love, the delicate maidenly blossoms to whom he chose to give his heart were usually of the type that leads a man up the garden path.

He fell in love with twelve women in all. Of these, nine, who had vowed never to take anyone but him, went off and married other men. That left three and of these, one ran off with someone else, another, in playful mood, poured vitriol over him by mistake and one - who unbeknown to him was a divorcee - went back to her husband.

Whatever he turned his hand to came out badly for him. He embarked on a career in the Civil Service, for example, and one day he left the office, got into some sort of crowd and before he knew what was happening, he had been arrested. At the police station, they found some stones in his pocket and he learned, to his amazement, that he had apparently been throwing stones at the dragoons. He got two months, lost his job in the Government Office, appealed against conviction and sentence and had the sentence raised to five months by the appeal court.

Then he set himself up as a dealer in cosmetics. He settled in a small town which counted among its nine hundred inhabitants eight hundred and twenty workers in a glass factory. Naturally enough, none of these good people bought his powders, his lotions for the complexion and delicate toilet-soaps, his perfumes and toothpastes and sweet-smelling ointments which made the breasts grow firmer and the hair thicker. So he sold it all for a song to a chemist in the main town of the district, where there was a military garrison, and before he could send the goods off, a fire broke out in his shop and the whole lot went up in a blazing inferno.

So off he went to the town to shoot himself. He went to a hotel, lay down on the bed, cocked the gun, pressed the trigger . . . and the bullet missed his head and went through the thin wooden partition into the adjoining room where it knocked a cup of tea out of the hand of a commercial traveller and smashed the sample bottles of liqueur in his suitcase. This gave rise to protracted and unpleasant complications, fines and claims for compensation. The hotel-owner behaved as if the unfortunate Mr Lindiger had shot the whole hotel to pieces and the commercial traveller blew his sample-bottles up into hectolitre vats of liqueur.

Small wonder then that, after all these afflictions and misfortunes, Mr Lindiger's face assumed an expression of infinite sadness.

One day, he read that as a result of the death of the owner, a large coffin-business was selling off its stock at a low price. It did not take Mr Lindiger long to make up his mind. He saw that dogged as he was at every step by ill-luck and misfortune, he was fated to become a trader in some thoroughly melancholy commodity.

And he quickly came to see the great advantages of the coffin-trade for here, after all, is a product for which there will always be customers.

'Well now,' he said to himself, 'I've already stood on the brink of death; why not take the plunge into coffins?' So he bought a stock of coffins of all shapes and sizes and looked round for a place where he could set up shop. An acquaintance of his told him that Dolní Opatrovice didn't yet have a wholesale and retail business of that kind and that furthermore, it was situated in an area with a harsh climate. So he applied for the concession, and three weeks later they were hanging up this sign outside a certain house in Dolní Opatrovice:

FRANTIŠEK LINDIGER

ACCREDITED DEALER
IN COFFINS OF ALL KINDS
FOR GENTLEMEN, LADIES
AND CHILDREN

Mr Lindiger had more than three hundred coffins in stock. He smiled as he walked up and down among them in his store-room. His heart was filled with gladness. Now at last he had a product that no-one could do without.

That evening, in the restaurant, he made the acquaintance of the leading figures of local society and his good humour became somewhat dented. For the conversation got round to the 'flu which was about that year and he complained of a certain tightness in the chest. 'You'll get better here,' said the Tax-Inspector, 'It's a very healthy area.'

'That's a blow, dammit!' sighed Mr Lindiger and his face clouded over.

A fortnight later, he was hanging his head. Not a single customer as yet. 'I have faith,' he said to himself; 'surely God will send me a death from somewhere!' After four weeks, he was looking like a ghost and vainly attempting to drum up some custom by means of a sign he had fixed to his door: 'ALSO AVAILABLE ON THE INSTALMENT PLAN'.

The people who walked by seemed to him to be bulging with muscle and bursting with health. He spent hours on end sitting in his shop and sighing: 'Great God Almighty, what a healthy area this is!'

At night, he dreamed of nothing but epidemics: of cholera, of spotted typhus and a doorway jammed with weeping widows and relatives. Forty coffins a day – fifty – whole families were dying off. He was about to send a telegram to a certain firm: 'Please send by return, high-speed freight, 1,200 coffins. Damaged goods accepted if necessary.' And then Mr Lindiger would awake from his beautiful dream, alone among his coffins, and no-one would come, no-one would open the door and ask him, in a voice choked with tears, to come and take the measurements.

He tried another tack. In the Club that night, when the beer was flowing, he started a conversation about the Chinese. The Chinese, he said, had a very keen awareness of the Last Things. Over there, the idea was to get yourself a handsome coffin while you were still alive. Husbands would buy their wives a coffin as a present; children would buy coffins for their parents.

He spoke with the tongue of an angel. He was warm in his praise of this custom and ended by saying that something of the kind ought to be brought in over here. He, for example, would start the ball rolling and would be glad to donate a fine oak coffin as a prize in the Charity Tombola which was to be held in a week's time. If this proved a success, he was willing to give away a small child's coffin free with every third coffin sold . . . The people looked uneasily at one another and then down at his beer-mat and finally, the organiser of this entertainment told him that the maximum weight of gift they were accepting for the tombola was one kilogram.

He went home in a state of dejection and overnight got together this poster, which he displayed in his window.

ABSOLUTELY FREE

To anyone buying a coffin from this shop

A

SPLENDID SHROUD IN PURE LINEN

Order a child's coffin, and get a free set of
Tasteful Decorative Pictures

Every tenth coffin free with bulk-orders.
Replacement of unsuitable coffins guaranteed.

'If that doesn't do the trick,' he said to himself, 'nothing will.' It didn't. He began to have hallucinations in which the funeral-bell was tolling. Every time, he would rush out and ask who had died, and every time he came home again disappointed.

Then it came to the point where he started speaking openly and in public about a brother of his who was a ship's doctor at present working in India where the plague was raging at the moment and saying that he had written to ask him to hurry up and pay him a visit.

In the pub, he took to saying that since it was winter now, it would do the children no end of good if their parents were to send them out into the snow barefoot, to toughen them up.

And then one day, his face lit up. A certain local inhabitant had been unfortunate enough to shoot himself in the stomach in a hunting-accident and it was said that he was not going to recover. He rubbed his hands and said that he would give the man a coffin the like of which Dolní Opatrovice had never seen.

That hope, too, was dashed. They took their fellow-townsman off to hospital in Prague, with Mr Lindiger running along behind the waggon for part of the way and shouting in desperation: 'Don't take him to Prague! I'll give you a fifty per cent discount!' His fears were realised: his hopes were laid to rest in Prague.

Then one night, there was an attack on the District Medical Officer, who had come to inoculate the children of school age. Someone knocked his top hat in. The general opinion was that it was Mr Lindiger who had done it. At the same time, an unsigned petition was received at the Sheriff's Office requesting that the Imperial and Royal Sheriff's Office should ban doctors from treating the sick.

This was on a Tuesday. On the Wednesday, the gendarme who had come to investigate the assault on the Medical Officer found Mr Lindiger hanging from a nail behind his door. Remarkably, his face wore a light-hearted expression, which was explained by the inscription written underneath the body: 'At least, that's one coffin off my hands!'

It was learned in addition that there was an unfinished letter on his desk in which he was planning to order twenty flasks of spotted typhus bacilli from the Bacteriological Institute in Vienna. Truly, this was a man with the real entrepreneurial spirit!

1914

The Bachura Scandal

Young Bachura, a Probationer Clerk in the City Council Offices, was an inexperienced soul who did not know that in the City Council a thousand dangers lie in wait for people of his sort and that a Probationer needs to be a man of strong character if he is not somehow to become entangled in a corruption scandal, either with or without the involvement of his superiors.

Probationer Bachura was not aware that hydra-headed Mammon lurks there, ready to swallow up the tender souls of Probationers, just as it has already swallowed that of many a grey-headed pillar of society.

None of the other great Town Hall scandals that have excited public opinion* can be put on a par with the Bachura Scandal.

Today, the tainted Bachura roams the world like Judas Iscariot, for he has soiled the pure banner of Public Administration anew, he has dragged it through the muck and the mire, he has . . . well, he has totally befouled it.

To get right to the heart of this story, we have to begin with that disgusting business in the Malá Strana.

Set in the tangled web of the narrow, old-fashioned streets of the Malá Strana, you will find the inn belonging to Mr Šedivý.

Mr Šedivý was one of those large, jolly old gentlemen who paid no heed to the health regulations laid down by the City Council of Prague and who had for decades, probably, had their air-pipes coming out in the urinal.

His customers never complained, for the beer was strong stuff and it was always dark in the urinal.

That urinal, which has such an important part to play in the Bachura Scandal, had no window giving onto the airshaft, no opening through which at least a gleam of God's good daylight could penetrate into this dark, dank place and bring into its gloom a little light and cheer.

But the beer-drinking patrons were quite happy, the conservative

* By which I do not mean *Public Opinion*, the journal edited by Mr Šašek. [J.H.]

Malá Strana, in its stony torpor, made no protest: an indifference to change sure to gladden the reactionary heart of Mr Luboš Jeřábek.

There came a day, however, when the mad rush of modern life burst even into Mr Šedivý's urinal.

The Buildings Department ascertained these two appalling facts: the air-pipes came out in the urinal (this was immediately passed on to the Public Health Department) and the urinal had no light and no outlet into the fresh air.

And that was how Probationer Clerk Bachura, in his capacity as a minute-clerk in the Buildings Department, first made the acquaintance of Mr Šedivý.

On the inspection visit, he returned a withering look to every one of Mr Šedivý's manoeuvres. The latter argued, robustly and defiantly, that people had been performing their minor bodily functions in this urinal before a single member of the august Buildings Department had been born. It was perfectly all right, he said: you didn't need to see what you were doing. As long as there was a channel to carry the water away, that was enough. There was a door, and that sufficed as an opening into the outside air.

'Just you calm down,' he was told, 'or you might end up insulting an official person. Do you think it's a joyride for us, going round looking into urinals?'

Then he was ordered to knock a hole in the urinal wall and put a window in and since this meant an alteration in a structure forming a part of licensed premises, he would have to submit plans and a request for permission to make this hole.

That was in the morning. In the afternoon, the people from the Public Health arrived. They ordered him to take the pipes through the opening (the opening having been made) into the airshaft.

He was driven half-way round the bend by all this. He had to make the hole as directed but he also had to submit a plan and a request for permission to make the hole and then, for health-reasons, take his air-pipes out into the airshaft, on to which the window of every toilet in the house opened.

He didn't sleep a wink that night, and next morning he went to the master-mason and asked him to draw up plans for a window, and using the services of a professional penman from the Hradčany, sent in a request to the august City Council for speedy approval of the plans drawn up in connection with his urinal and for permission to knock a hole in the wall of said urinal, the which being granted, he promised to show his gratitude by the exemplary behaviour of his declining years. Three weeks went by and no decision on his request had arrived. So innkeeper Šedivý betook himself to the City Council, to press for more urgent action. In the Buildings Department he found only Probationer Bachura, since all the others had been in the Corinth Restaurant over the road since nine o'clock, having a snack. It was now precisely twelve.

'What can I do for you?' asked Bachura in a lofty tone.

'Well, young man, I've come about that urinal of mine. Šedivý, you know, the urinal in the Malá Strana.'

'Oh yes, I remember,' said Bachura in a lordly manner. 'I do seem to recall something about that. But what exactly is it that you want?'

'Well, you see, it's been three weeks now and it would be very nice if you could speed things up a bit. My customers are looking forward to having that window as eagerly as little children. Nothing much happens down our way and it would be an event.'

Bachura recalled that the request had already been processed and was lying ready in a drawer. It needed only to be sent off. But the Head of Section had said to him: 'Don't send it yet. It's only an innkeeper: let him wait a bit. We in the City Council have got to keep these people firmly in their place.'

He was silent for a while and then said: 'Well, we'll see what we can do.'

Two weeks later, innkeeper Šedivý was back again and for a second time, Bachura pronounced with pompous solemnity: 'Well, we'll see what we can do.'

About a week after this last encounter, Bachura was walking along the František Embankment, not on official business, but to keep a rendezvous with a certain young lady who was delighted to have a young man who worked in the City Council.

It was a lovely afternoon, warm with a clear sky. Bachura stopped at the soft-drinks kiosk and bought himself a raspberry- and a lemonade and walked on with his mind full of longing thoughts about the girl whom he was shortly to meet.

There on the horizon was Hradčany; the Petřín Gardens were swathed in greenery, the chestnuts were in blossom on Střelecký Island. But in the middle of all this beauty, he began to feel the pangs of bellyache. Before leaving home, Bachura had eaten a glass of yoghurt, the national dish of our defeated enemies, the Bulgarians. The raspberry and lemon drinks had put the finishing touches to the process which was progressing on its inexorable path through the intestinal labyrinth of the Probationer-Clerk from the City Council.

In the gardens on the embankment opposite the Hradčany, there stands a little building. Such a tiny structure, and yet it towers in significance above all the others in the vicinity. 'Often a tiny shepherd's hut can do more good than the mighty camp where warlike Žižka stood': words that come into my mind every time I pass that humble cot.

It bears two inscriptions. From the embankment you can see the word 'GENTLEMEN', and from the children's playground in the park which borders the embankment, the more discreet message 'LADIES'.

Bachura burst into it like a roaring lion, like an Arab hurling himself on a spring in an oasis or a recruiting-sergeant on a potential new recruit.

'Number One, or Number Two?'

'Two,' said Bachura, shyly but hastily.

The Latrine-Lady took a look at him and said: 'I know you from somewhere, young sir.' She tore off a ticket. Bachura dipped into his purse and exclaimed in dismay: 'It can't be! I was sure I still had change.'

The old girl looked at him again and said slowly, dragging out the agony of Bachura's predicament: 'Do you know where I know you from? From that time you came to see my brother Šedivý, the innkeeper in the Malá Strana. I was home that day when you came with those officials who were on about our urinal. Go on, here's a ticket for you; I'm sure it won't be wasted on you.'

Bachura leaped into the little cubicle and when he emerged, a happy and carefree man, the old woman called after him: 'And you won't forget, will you, sir, to sort out that little matter of my brother's toilet?'

The first thing Bachura did next day, without asking his superior's permission, was to send off the decision on that request for the authorisation of his plans, which had been lying about ready for the last five weeks, to Mr Šedivý and heave a sigh of contentment.

Every morning, before nine o'clock, Councillor Staněk from the Town Hall was in the habit of dropping in at that little house on the František Embankment where Probationer Bachura had committed his disgraceful act of corruption, to have a chat with the Latrine-Lady and bring himself up to date on what the public thought of the city administration. For him, the Lady of the Latrines was the Voice of the

People. It was a little quirk of his.

'Well, I dunno, Your Honour, this corruption-lark seems to be spreading down to the juniors as well,' expatiated the old dear. 'These people from the Town Hall, if you let them do it for nothing, they're at your service. Like the time my brother . . .'

And she related the story of Probationer Bachura's corruption to the Councillor in all its horrific detail.

Today, another Probationer is sitting where once Bachura sat. When the official disciplinary investigation, in which he was found guilty of taking a bribe in the matter of the innkeeper Šedivý, was over, he was dismissed from the Council's service.

Now he wanders about Europe like a Judas. He was last seen in Hamburg, staring in a suspicious manner into the black waters of the canal.

Someone overheard him talking to himself: 'If only I'd bought a subscription ticket for a whole year! Oh dear, oh dear! . . . It's always the little villains that they hang!'

1914

The Cynological Institute

I

Ever since I can remember, I have had a fondness for animals, of whatever kind. At a tender age, I used to bring mice home and once, when I was missing school, I went through the whole period playing with a dead cat.

.I took an interest in snakes as well. There was one time that I caught a snake on a stony hillside in a forest and was going to take it away with me to put it into my Aunt Anna's bed (I didn't like her). Fortunately, the gamekeeper came on the scene and he identified it as a viper and killed it and took it away to claim the official reward. Between the ages of eighteen and twenty-four, my inclinations lay towards animals of really substantial bulk, with a particular predilection for camels and elephants of all kinds.

This interest gradually waned and between twenty-four and twenty-eight, cattle and horses began to attract my attention. I fancied the idea of a stud, or of a breeding-herd of Siamese cattle. This turned out to be mere wishful thinking and I was left with no alternative but to transfer my affections to animals of smaller breeds. I gave dogs precedence over cats and when I reached the age of thirty, certain differences arose between me and my relatives. They reproached me with the fact that I did not have a proper job and had so far made no effort to stand on my own feet. I arrived at my decision quickly; I announced to my nearest and dearest that as a dog-lover, I was going into the dog-trade.

It is worthy of note that they derived no pleasure from this announcement.

II

If a man is going to set up in business, there is no question but that he must do so under a designation which makes it abundantly clear what business he is setting up in. The common designation of 'dog-dealer' did not, however, appeal to me, in view of the fact that a certain distant relative of mine works in the Ministry and he would have objected to it.

The simple legend: 'Dogs for Sale' did not appeal to me either, for I had it in mind to carry on my trade at a rather higher level. In the Scientific Dictionary, I came across the term 'cynology', which means the science of dogs. Then I walked past the Agricultural Institute and that did it. I conferred on my establishment the title of 'Cynological Institute'. It was a proud, a learned title denoting, as I indicated in my large advertisements, 'the breeding and sale and purchase and exchange of dogs on cynological principles.'

These large advertisements, in which the expression 'Cynological Institute' was repeated so often, left me speechless with wonder myself. There I was at last, the proprietor of an *Institute*! No-one who has not experienced it for himself can know the pride, the magic that lies in that word. In the advertisements, I had undertaken to provide expert advice on all matters pertaining to dogs. Anyone buying a dozen dogs, I announced, would get one puppy as a free gift. A dog, I went on, is the ideal thing as a gift for a birthday, a confirmation or an engagement, or as a present for a wedding or a jubilee. For a child, a dog was a toy that could not easily get broken or torn. A faithful guide which will not attack you in the forest. All breeds of dog in stock. Direct contacts with abroad. A training-establishment attached for dogs that were badly behaved. In my Cynological Institute, the fiercest dog would be cured of snapping and barking within a fortnight. Where to put the dog when you went on holiday? In the Cynological Institute. Where to get your dog trained to sit up and beg within three days? In the Cynological Institute.

On reading these advertisements, an uncle of mine shook his head apprehensively and said: 'No, no, lad, you're not well. Don't you sometimes feel a pain at the back of your head?'

I, however, looked to the future with hope and without having as yet acquired a single dog, waited eagerly for an order of some kind and advertised for an assistant of honest character and good behaviour who was not currently liable for military service and would not have to go back into the army until the dogs had had time to win their way into his affections.

III

My advertisement for a 'Man to assist in the breeding and sale of dogs' brought in a whole sheaf of replies, some of which showed a great deal of frankness. One retired country policeman wrote that if he got the post, he would teach all the dogs to jump over sticks and walk on their heads.

Another wrote that he knew how to handle dogs, for he had worked for years for the knacker in Budějovice and had been discharged on account of the gentle way in which he had handled the dead animals.

One applicant confused 'Cynological' with 'Gynaecological' and wrote that he had worked in a maternity hospital and in clinics for women's diseases.

Fifteen applicants had completed courses in law, twelve were qualified teachers. In addition, I received a communication from the Society for Aid to Former Prisoners saying that with regard to the post of assistant, I need look no further; they had just the man for me, a former convicted safebreaker. Some applications struck a very sad and hopeless note. Many began by writing themselves: 'Although I know in advance that I will not get this job . . .'

Among this plethora of applicants, there were those who knew Spanish, English, French, Turkish, Russian, Polish, Croat, German, Hungarian and Danish. One screed was even written in Latin.

And then came a simple and frank request: 'Dear Sir, When do I start? Yours Respectfully, Ladislav Čížek, c/o Medřický, Košíře.' When an applicant approaches you as directly as that, there is nothing for it but to write and tell him to come on Wednesday at eight a.m. I felt myself under a deep obligation to him for having spared me the long and onerous business of selection.

And so on Wednesday, at eight o'clock, my assistant started work. He was a slightly-built, pock-marked, very lively man who, when he first saw me, grasped me by the hand and said gaily: 'It doesn't look as if the weather will perk up till tomorrow . . . did you hear that another two trams collided in Pilsen Street at seven this morning?'

Then he took a short-stemmed pipe out of his pocket and told me that he had got it from the chauffeur at Stibrals' and that he smoked Hungarian tobacco. He next informed me that at a place he knew in Nusle there was a waitress called Pepina and asked whether we hadn't by any chance been at school together. Then he began to talk about a certain dachshund which would need to be dyed a different colour if I were to buy it, and to have its legs bent a little.

'You know about dogs, then?' I asked joyfully.

'Do I know about dogs? I've been in the business myself and already tangled with the law over it. One time I was taking a boxer home and out of the blue, a man stops me in the street and says this is his dog and he lost it on Ovocná Street two hours ago. "How do you know it's your dog?" "By the fact that its name is Mupo. Here, Mupo!" You wouldn't believe the joy with which that dog jumped up at him. "Bosko," I called out to him. "Bosko, for shame!" So he came dashing merrily back to me. Thick as two short planks, that dog was. The worst thing was, I forgot, when the case came to court, that I'd called him Bosko on that occasion. But he answered to "Laddie" as well and was just as pleased to see me. Would you like me to look round for a dog for you?'

'No, Čížek, I'm going to run my business on very practical lines. We'll wait for a customer and while we're waiting, we'll look through the advertisements in the Animals columns to see who's selling, and what kind of dog. Look, here's a lady who wants to sell a year-old white spitz for lack of space. Is a spitz really so big that it needs that much space? Off you go now to Školská Street and buy him. Here's thirty crowns.'

He parted from me with the assurance that he'd be back in no time, but it was three hours before he returned . . . and what a state he was in! He had his hard hat rammed down over his ears and was teetering alarmingly from side to side like a man on the deck of a ship during a storm at sea. Gripped tight in one hand, he held a piece of rope, which he was dragging behind him. I looked at the end of the rope. There was nothing there.

'Well now . . . h-h-how do you like him? . . . nice little chap, eh? . . . it's taken . . . a bit longer than I thought' (he began to hiccup and collided with the door) '. . . look at his ears . . . come on then, nitwit . . . dig your toes in, would you? . . . she was very reluctant to sell him . . .'

He turned round as he said this and looked at the end of the rope. He rubbed his eyes, took hold of the end, fumbled with it and hiccupped: 'I-i-it was there an hour ago!'

He sat down on a chair, fell off it straight away and pulling himself up on my legs into a standing position, said triumphantly, as if he had made some fabulous discovery: 'It looks as if that dog of ours has run off.' He sat down on the chair and began to snore.

And that was how he began work in my employ.

I looked out of the window onto the street. There, amid the hustle and bustle, a variety of dogs were running about. Every one of them, so it seemed to me, was for sale while this fellow beside me was snoring his head off. I tried to wake him, for I had the *idée fixe* that a customer would come along and want to buy not one, but a whole dozen dogs. But nobody came and it was a waste of time trying to wake him up, as well. All I achieved was that he slid out of the chair. Three hours later, he at last awoke of his own accord and said in a hoarse voice, as he rubbed his eyes: 'I have the feeling I've done something wrong.'

He began to recall individual details and went on at length about the spitz, what a pretty dog it had been and how cheaply that lady had sold it to him. He had given ten crowns for it, having told her that it was going to a very good home. Then he related how the dog had not wanted to come with him and how he had beaten it. He then made an abrupt leap to the point that he had an acquaintance who kept a pub down in Smíchov and so he had dropped in on him. There had been a number of other people there that he knew. They'd had a glass or two of wine and of spirits. A very frail vessel is man.

'All right then,' I said, 'you were given thirty crowns, as you know. Give me back the other twenty.'

This did not throw him off his stroke in the slightest. 'It's true, I should have given you back twenty crowns, but I thought I'd give you a nice surprise. So I called round at Švihanec as well and there I put down a deposit of ten crowns for some puppies with a bloke called Kratký. They've got such an odd-looking, interesting bitch there and she'll be having a litter soon. We'll be really keen to see what kind of pups she turns out. The main thing is, we've already got them secured. Then I went along to Paliárka; there's a lovely doe for sale there . . .'

'Wait a minute, Čížek, I'm not in the rabbit-trade, you know.'

'Did I say doe?' said my assistant. 'That was a mistake. I meant a Scottish sheepdog bitch. She's going to have pups as well, but I didn't put down the ten crowns on the puppies; they were just an advance on the bitch. The owner will keep the pups and we'll send for the bitch when she's had them. Then I went down Krocínová Street . . .'

'But you didn't have any money left by then.'

'Yes, that's true, I hadn't any money left by then. If I had had some money, then there's a Mr Novák there who has a large shaggy dog for sale and I'd have put it down as a deposit, so that we could have it at our disposal. Well, I'll just get myself sorted out now, and go over to Školská Street. That spitz is sure to have got home by now, after it ran away from me. I'll be back with it within the hour.'

Čížek was true to his word. He returned in less than an hour, completely sober and out of breath. To my great surprise, he had brought along a black spitz.

'You just can't get it right, can you?' I exclaimed. 'That lady did say in her advertisement that it was a white spitz she wanted to sell.'

For a while, he stared at the dog in a puzzled manner, then ran off with it, without saying a word.

Two hours later, he was back with a white spitz, which was in a desperately dirty and muddy state and behaved in a terribly ferocious manner.

'That business about the spitz was all a mistake,' said Čížek. 'That there lady down in that Školská Street in Prague had two spitzes, a black one and a white one. She was very pleased when I brought her that black one back.'

I looked at the identification-mark on the one he had brought. It was from the Žižkov district. Suddenly, the feeling came over me that I wanted to cry, but I got myself under control. (Čížek, meanwhile, had removed the identification-mark, saying that they were dangerous things.)

That night, I was awakened by a scratching at the door. I opened it, and the black spitz, my old acquaintance from the previous afternoon, burst into the flat, barking joyfully. Perhaps it had been missing us, or maybe it was just too long a way for it to go home. Whatever the reason, I now had two dogs; all I needed was a customer.

IV

The customer arrived at about ten o'clock in the morning. He looked round the flat and asked: 'Where do you keep your dogs, then?'

'I don't keep them at home,' I said. 'Apart from two spitzes, which I'm training and which are already promised to the Archduke in Brandeis. I keep my dogs in the country, with a view to ensuring that they get fresh air and don't pick up vermin, or the measles, which not even the most careful dog-dealer in the city can guard against. It is a principle of our Cynological Institute that our dogs should be provided with the opportunity to run free and so out in the country, where we have our kennels, the keeper disperses them all over the area and the dogs don't come back till evening.

'This also has the advantage that it teaches them to stand on their own feet, for during the day, they seek out their own food. We have leased large tracts of land for them, where they can feed on all kinds of game and you really ought to see the fun when one of those tiny ratters is fighting with a hare.'

The gentleman was very pleased by this, for he nodded his head and said:

'So you'll have some nice fierce dogs for sale, then, trained as guard-dogs.'

'Oh, certainly. We've got dogs on our books that are so terrifying that I can't even let you have a photograph of them. They would have torn the photographer limb from limb. I've got dogs that have already torn criminals apart.'

'That's just the kind of dog I'm after,' said the customer. 'I've got a timber-yard and now that it's winter, I'd like to get hold of a good guard-dog. Could you get one in from your kennels for me by tomorrow afternoon, so that I can come and have a look at him?'

'Why certainly, Sir. No trouble at all. I'll send my man for him straight away. Čížek!'

He appeared wearing an ingratiating smile and made it known straight away that he thought he'd seen the gentleman somewhere before.

'Čížek', I said, making a sign to him, 'go and get that really vicious guard-dog of ours. What's his name, again?'

'Fabian,' said Čížek, without batting an eyelid. 'His mother was called "Witch"; a fearsome dog that is. It's already savaged and eaten two children because they gave it to them to play with by mistake and they tried to climb on its back. Now, as far as the deposit is concerned . . .'

'Oh, of course!' said the customer. 'Here's forty crowns as a deposit. What's his price?'

'A hundred crowns,' said Čížek, 'and a gulden extra on his tail. We also have a cheaper one at eighty crowns, but he's only bitten off three of a man's fingers, when he tried to stroke him.'

'I'll take the more vicious one.'

And so Čížek set off with the forty crowns' deposit to look for a guard-dog and he came back in the evening with a sad-looking, broken-down specimen.

'But that's a real dish-rag!' I cried in astonishment.

'Cheap, though,' said Čížek. 'I met a butcher who was just taking him off to the knacker's. Said he wouldn't pull any more and that he was starting to bite. So I reckon he'll make a first-class guard-dog. Anyway, if the thief knows what he's about, he'll poison it and that gent will be round to buy another from us.'

We spent some time arguing about this and then Čížek gave the dog a thorough combing and we cooked it a meal of rice and sinews. He ate two pots full of this, after which he looked just as listless and miserable as he had before. He licked our boots, walked about the room without taking an interest in anything and you could see that he was annoyed that his master had not got him as far as the knacker's yard.

Čížek tried one more trick to turn him into a ferocious creature. Because that dog was brownish-white, in effect grey in colour, he got some Indian ink and painted large black stripes across the body, which made him look like a hyena.

The gentleman, when he came to get him next day, stepped back in horror when he saw him.

'That's a fearsome beast,' he cried.

'He won't hurt anyone who belongs to the family. "Fox" is his name; go on, just try him out, give him a stroke.'

The customer feared for his safety, so we literally had to lead him up to the ugly brute and force him to stroke it. The guard-dog began to lick his hand and went off with him like a lamb.

And before morning, that gentleman had been comprehensively burgled.

V

Christmas was coming. In the meantime, we had turned the black spitz into a golden spitz by the application of an oxide lotion and made the black spitz into a white one by painting it with a solution of silver nitrate. Both dogs howled fearfully during this operation, which gave the impression that the Cynological Institute had at least sixty dogs at its disposal, instead of just two.

But we made up for this by our profusion of puppies. Čížek, to all appearances, suffered from the delusion that puppies were the key to prosperity and so, as Christmas approached, he kept on arriving with the pockets of his winter overcoat stuffed full of nothing but puppies. I would send him out to get a mastiff and he would bring me dachshund puppies. I would send him out for a pinscher, and he would bring me a fox-terrier pup. We had thirty puppies in all and had put down deposits for a hundred and twenty more.

I had the idea of leasing a shop, in preparation for the holiday season, in Ferdinandová Street in Prague, setting up a Christmas tree there and selling the puppies, decorated with pretty bright-coloured ribbons, under the slogan: 'Make your children really happy this Christmas by buying them a healthy puppy.'

I hired the shop. This was about a week before Christmas.

'Čížek,' I said, 'take the puppies down to our shop in Prague, buy a nice big tree and put the puppies in an attractive display. Get some moss. In a word, I'm relying on you to do the whole thing in the best of taste. Got it?'

'You bet. I'll give you a real treat.' He put the puppies in boxes and loaded them into a handcart, and that afternoon I went down to take a look at this treat he had in store for me and to see how nicely and tastefully he had arranged his window-display.

The crowd of people in front of the shop told me that the puppies had aroused enormous interest. But as I came closer, I heard cries of outrage from among the throng. 'I've never seen anything so barbarous. What are the police doing? I'm amazed that something like this can be allowed.'

When I pushed my way through to the display-window, it's a wonder my legs didn't give way under me.

Čížek's pretty arrangement had consisted of hanging two dozen puppies on the branches of the Christmas tree as if they had been bags of sweets. The poor creatures were dangling there with their tongues hanging out like thieves hanging from a tree in the Middle Ages . . . And underneath stood the inscription: 'Make your children really happy this Christmas by buying them a healthy, adorable little puppy.'

That was the finish of my Cynological Institute.

1914

The Emperor Franz Joseph's Portrait

In Mladá Boleslav there lived a stationer called Petiška. He was a man who respected the law and had lived, for longer than anyone could remember, across the road from the barracks. On the Emperor's birthday and other Imperial and Royal occasions, he would hang out a black-and-gold banner from his house and provide Chinese lanterns for the Officers' Club. He sold pictures of Franz Joseph to gin shops in the Mladá Boleslav area and to the police station. He would have supplied portraits of Our Ruler to the schools under the administration of the local education authority as well, but the dimensions of his pictures did not conform to the specifications approved by the Regional Schools Council. 'I'm sorry, Mr Petiška,' the Imperial and Royal Regional School Inspector said to him once when they met in the Sheriff's Office, 'but you're trying to give us a longer and wider Emperor than the one prescribed in the Regional Schools Council Instruction of 20th October 1891. The Emperor as defined in the Instruction is somewhat shorter. Only Emperors 48 cm high and 36 cm wide are permitted. Your Emperor is 50 cm high and 40 cm wide. You reply that you have two thousand pictures of our Monarch in stock. Don't imagine that you're going to fob off any old rubbish onto us. Your Emperor is shoddy goods through and through. And the way they've got him up is a scandal. He looks as if his whiskers have never been combed, there's an enormous splash of red on his nose and on top of it all, he's got a squint.'

When Mr Petiška got home, he said irritably to his wife: 'That old Emperor of ours has landed us in a pretty pickle!' And this was before the war had started. Mr Petiška had been lumbered, in short, with two thousand portraits of the Emperor. When war did break out, Mr Petiška was overjoyed and full of high hopes of shifting that merchandise of his. He displayed pictures of the bloodthirsty old codger in his shop under the inscription: 'A good buy! The Emperor Franz Joseph for 15 crowns!' He sold six: five to the barracks, where these lithographed portraits of the Last of the Habsburgs were hung up in the canteens to whip up the fervour of the reservists, and one which was bought by old Šimr, the tobacconist. This Austrian patriot beat him down to 12 crowns and still complained in heartfelt tones that it was daylight robbery.

He took out advertisements and offered the Emperor for sale in *National Politics* and *Voice of the People*: 'In these difficult days, no Czech home should be without its portrait of our sorely tried Monarch, at 15 crowns'. He didn't get any orders, but he did get a summons to present himself at the District Sheriff's Office, where he was informed that in future, he had better avoid expressions like 'difficult days' and 'sorely tried'. Instead, he should use: 'glorious days' and 'victorious'. Otherwise, he would find himself involved in complications. So he issued the following advertisement: 'In these glorious days, no Czech home should be without its portrait of our victorious Monarch, at 15 crowns'. But that didn't work either.

All he received was a number of obscene communications, in which his anonymous correspondents advised him with total frankness to put his portraits of the Emperor where the monkey keeps its nuts, and yet another invitation to the Sheriff's Office, where the Duty Commissar told him that he must follow the guide-lines issued by the Imperial and Royal Correspondence Office in the wording of his advertisements. 'The Russians are in Hungary, they've captured Lvov and got as far as Přemyšl. You don't talk about "glorious days" in the face of all that, Mr Petiška. It sounds as if you are amusing yourself, indulging in sarcasm and irony. With adverts like that, you could end up in the Castle, in front of a Court Martial.'

Mr Petiška promised that he would be careful and composed the following advertisement: 'Every Czech would be glad to sacrifice 15 crowns for the opportunity to hang our aged Monarch in his home.' The local journals refused to take the advertisement. 'Good God, man,' said one Managing Editor to him, 'do you want to get us all shot?'

Mr Petiška went home very upset. At the back of his shop the parcels containing his stock of Emperor's portraits were lying about all over the place. Mr Petiška dipped into one and was horrified by what he found. He looked round anxiously and was relieved to discover that no one had seen him. He began gloomily to brush the dust off the parcel and found that some were damp and mouldy. His black tomcat was sitting behind the parcels. There could be no shadow of doubt as to who was responsible for their moist condition. In an attempt to divert suspicion from itself, the cat began to purr. Mr Petiška threw a broom at the treasonous animal, and it fell silent. In a rage the stationer stormed into the living quarters and growled at his wife: 'That bloody animal has got to go! Who's going to buy an Emperor that's been pee'd on by a cat? The Emperor's mouldy. He'll have to be dried out, God dammit!'

Mr Petiška's afternoon nap, which he took while his wife was looking after the shop, was very disturbed. He imagined that the police had come for the black tomcat and that he, too, was being taken along with it before a Court Martial. Then it seemed as if he and the cat had been sentenced to death by hanging and that the cat was the first to go. And he, Petiška, was blaspheming at the Court in terrible language. He gave a fearsome shout – and saw his wife standing beside him. 'Heavens above!' she said to him reproachfully. 'The language you're using! If someone were to hear you like this!'

She reported in an agitated voice that she had in the meantime tried to dry the Emperor in the garden, but that some stone-throwing hooligans had used him for target-practice 'and now he looks like a sieve.'

Other losses were registered as well. The hens had come and sat on one picture of the Emperor, which was drying on the grass, while they were going through their digestive processes and in the condition they were in, had turned his whiskers green. The young Saint Bernard belonging to Holeček, the butcher, which was a naïve young thing and had no knowledge of Paragraph 63 of the Criminal Code, had attempted to eat two pictures. That pup had it in its blood, though. Its mother had been destroyed by the knacker a year ago for eating the banner of the 36th Regiment on the parade ground.

Mr Petiška was not a happy man. In the wine-cellar that evening, he said something about a 'good buy' and about the difficulties he was having with the Emperor. The burden of his speech was that the authorities in Vienna looked on the Czechs with distrust because they weren't buying portraits of the Monarch, at 15 crowns a time, from the firm of František Petiška in Mladá Boleslav.

'Bring the price down,' said the landlord, when it was closing time. 'These are hard times. Horejsek is selling his steam-thresher for 300 crowns less than he gave for it last year and the Emperor's in the same boat.'

And so Mr Petiška wrote out the following announcement and put it in the display-case in his shop window: 'In view of the economic crisis, I am offering a large number of beautiful portraits of the Emperor, normally priced at 15 crowns, for 10 crowns each.'

And once more all was quiet in the shop. 'How's the Emperor going?' asked our friend the owner of the wine-cellar. 'Poorly,' replied Mr Petiška. 'There's no demand for the Emperor.'

'If I were you, you know,' said the landlord of the wine-cellar in a confidential tone, 'I'd try to get rid of him at any price, before it's too late.'

'I'll wait a bit longer,' said Mr Petiška.

And so the ill-disciplined black tomcat continued to sprawl all over the portraits of the Emperor. After eighteen months, the mould had even reached the Emperors at the bottom of the pile. The Austrians were on the way out and Austria as a whole was like something the cat had brought in.

And then Mr Petiška took paper and pencil and worked out with a heavy heart that he wasn't going to get rich this way and that if he sold the Emperor for two crowns he'd still make a crown on each portrait.

And he devised some effective publicity. He put a portrait in the display case and wrote underneath: 'This ancient Monarch reduced from 15 to 2 crowns.'

All Mladá Boleslav came that same day to Mr Petiška's shop, to see how shares in the Habsburg dynasty had suddenly fallen through the floor.

And that night the police came for Mr Petiška, and after that things moved swiftly. They shut up the shop and they shut up Mr Petiška and brought him before a Court Martial for committing an offence against public peace and order. The Ex-Servicemen's Society expelled him at an Extraordinary Plenary Session.

Mr Petiška got thirteen months' hard labour. He should really have got five years, but it was argued in mitigation that he had once fought for Austria at the Battle of Custozza. And the parcels of portraits of the Emperor have been impounded in the meanwhile in the military depository in Terezína, awaiting the hour of liberation when, on the liquidation of Austria, some enterprising tradesman will wrap his cheeses in them.

1916